STAGE FRIGHT

STAGE FRIGHT

GILLIAN LINSCOTT

St. Martin's Press
New York

Library of Congress Cataloging-in-Publication Data

Linscott, Gillian.
State fright / Gillian Linscott.
p.   cm.
ISBN 0-312-09812-X
1. Bray, Nell (Fictitious character)—Fiction.   2. Women
detectives—England—Fiction.   3. Shaw, Bernard,
1856–1950—Fiction.   4. Dramatists, English—Fiction.
I. Title.
PR6062.I54S73   1993
823'.914—dc20   93-29098   CIP

First published in Great Britain by Little,
Brown and Company.

First U.S. Edition: December 1993
10 9 8 7 6 5 4 3 2 1

ONE

THE PROBLEMS OF THE PENWARDINES' marriage and the murder of the Lord Chamberlain's man at the Crispin Theatre should have been outside my social circles. I was involved because in the course of one evening in November 1909 I made two serious mistakes. The first was to accept an invitation to one of my aunt's soirées. The second was to pick up a postcard from George Bernard Shaw.

Of those, the soirée was the worse mistake because I should have known better. I did know better even as I replied to the invitation, but for once I let family feeling get the better of me, always an error and particularly so with this aunt. I don't like my mother's sister and she doesn't like me. She disapproved of my education, my manners, my politics and the fact that, in the year in question, I'd already spent two terms in Holloway for Suffragette activities. But in my aunt's world blood is thicker even than prison clothing. I could imagine the set of her formidable jaw as she penned my name on one of a stack of embossed invitation cards:

Mrs James Kilton. At home 6.30 to 8.30 pm.

Home for my aunt is a tall house in Knightsbridge, packed with paintings and china and large pieces of furniture that have come down from grander homes and sit brooding about it. I arrived on time, having to go on to a meeting afterwards, and was one of the first in my aunt's receiving line.

'Nell, I'm so very glad you could come.'

1

Her kiss was frostbite on my cheek. As I straightened up she whispered: 'Really, you might have changed.'

'I have changed, Aunt.'

My grey suit with the black braid was perfectly respectable. Besides, I could hardly go on to a meeting of the prisoners' support committee in the sort of clothes most of her women guests were wearing: velvet and second-best jewels. I accepted a glass of dry sherry from a hired footman and wondered who would be the least boring person to talk to in the statutory half hour before I could escape.

It was a close-run thing and I eventually selected the tall man with dark, receding hair and a head rather too large for his body, not because he seemed especially interesting but because he was standing on his own by a bookcase looking as gloomy as a wet rock while the party eddied round him. He was in his mid-thirties, so smoothly clean-shaven that he must have come fresh from the hands of barber or valet. He had the air of a man enduring with quiet dignity a lifetime of privilege. His eyes were roving round the room but apart from that he was as still as if practising to be a statue of himself. I had an idea that he was somebody I should recognise, probably a politician. As I walked up to him, his eyes turned to me with mild alarm in them.

'Well, it looks as if the Lords are going to throw out the people's Budget. That should mean an interesting few weeks in the Commons.'

I thought even my aunt could hardly object to that as a conversational opening. Assuming him to be an MP, it would offend neither Liberal nor Conservative.

'Oh yes. Yes, certainly.'

Still the alarm. Obviously he wasn't used to women trying to talk politics to him before they were introduced.

'I'm Nell Bray, niece of our hostess. Don't you think it's a ridiculous anachronism that a non-elected chamber can hold up a Budget?'

I hoped he'd follow my example and introduce himself, but he didn't.

He murmured: 'Certainly some people seem to think so.'

If that was the best he could do I'd certainly chosen the

wrong man. It became a challenge to get a reaction out of him. Tact began to slip.

'If the Lords go on obstructing the Budget, the Prime Minister will have to swamp the house with new peers. I've a proposal on how he should do it.'

'Oh yes?'

'For every peer in the Lords, the Government appoints his cook a peeress.'

'His . . . his cook, did you say?'

At last I'd got a reaction. He gulped. One eyebrow distinctly quivered.

'His cook. Achieving three things. Firstly we introduce women into Parliament, secondly some working people, thirdly we strike a blow at the heredity principle which at present means the breeding of our legislators is carried out rather less efficiently than the breeding of our racehorses.'

He'd gone quite pink and a muscle in his cheek was twitching. Conservative definitely. But there was clearly going to be no sensible argument out of him and I was relieved when I saw a woman friend of my aunt's I actually liked coming through the door. I asked him to excuse me and crossed the room to meet her.

'I see you've been doing your social duty, Nell.'

'Heavy duty. I seem to have picked the dullest man here.'

'Well, Lord Penwardine does have rather a lot on his mind at the moment.'

The look on my face told her.

'Oh Nell, you haven't been tactless again, have you?'

'I don't know if you'd call it tactless. I said his cook should be made a member of the House of Lords.'

'His cook?'

'All their cooks. I also told him that peers weren't as carefully bred as racehorses.'

Her expression changed from hilarity to concern. 'Oh dear. You know they're desperate for an heir? His wife wouldn't give him children and now she's gone and bolted. Surely you heard about that.'

'My dear Jeanie, I've better things to do with my time

3

than brood about the marital problems of the aristocracy.'

She gave a quick glance round to see if anybody was overhearing us.

'Oh dear, it looks as if he's telling Mummy about you already.'

I glanced over my shoulder. The man was talking to a woman with pewter-grey hair, their heads close together. She was not tall but there was a square set about shoulders and jaw that showed she wasn't used to being overlooked. Her hair was piled into an elaborate style that seemed to be held in place by pure willpower and she wore a heavy choker of pearls and opals in an upright, military way as if that were part of life's duties. As I glanced at her she put a lorgnette to her eyes, directed at me. My status, I thought, would be about that of an amoeba under a microscope.

Jeanie said: 'The dowager Marchioness of Penwardine is a great friend of your aunt's.'

'She would be. What about him?'

Since they were talking about me I thought it was fair enough to talk about them. Jeanie took a deep breath.

'You know he married an American heiress for the money to keep up the estate after his father had lost it all gambling?'

'I vaguely remember.'

'Orphan of a rail-road millionaire, red-haired but quite pretty. She brought him two million dollars when they married. That was six or seven years ago.'

'But it wasn't a success?'

'Well, obviously it wasn't a love match, at least not from his point of view, but she seemed to be adapting. Of course, Mummy was a problem. She expected a son and heir nine months after the honeymoon and was furious when Isabella didn't oblige.'

'Entirely her own fault, of course.'

'That was probably what made Isabella bolt in the end.'

'Bolting, of course, being very bad behaviour in a breeding heifer.'

Jeanie gave me a look that said I shouldn't go too far.

'She left him just after Ascot. She's set up home on her own in London and taken up with a fast set. She's

4

supposed to be having an affair with an actor. Charles Courts, the one who keeps crashing flying machines.'

'I've seen him. He's a good actor.'

'As well as being the best-looking man in Europe. I suppose sooner or later Lord Penwardine will divorce her. It's common knowledge that he's been in love with another woman for years, the proverbial childhood sweetheart, and when it comes to the son-and-heir stakes, time is ticking on.'

I knew I shouldn't lose my temper with Jeanie, who was the best of the bunch, but this was too much.

'He'll divorce her! He married the woman for her money, he's in love with somebody else but he can do the divorcing and his wife can't.'

'Shh. If I let you start on your speech about the divorce laws your aunt will never speak to me again. I know they're unfair on women, but what can you do about it?'

Deftly she roped in a couple of other women who happened to be passing and started a conversation about a Chopin recital they'd all attended. I hadn't, so I stayed for a minute longer and escaped, thanking my aunt on the way out. From the way she looked at me she already knew about my conversation with Lord Penwardine.

Outside it was dark and drizzling. I caught a horse tram to the meeting of the suffrage prisoners' support committee in St Pancras. It was well into its second combative hour when a postcard was passed to me hand to hand along the table. George Bernard Shaw, sitting at the far end, followed its progress. I read:

Nell,
Is it more useful to solve a murder or to prevent one?

That meant somebody in the suffrage movement must have been gossiping. I'd already had one brush with murder that year and it had been enough for me. I glanced along the table but Shaw, red beard propped on interlaced fingers, seemed intent on what somebody was telling us about problems of fund-raising. I turned the card over and wrote on the back:

It would depend on the identity of the intended victim.

I could think off-hand of several dozen people I wouldn't rush to save, beginning with my aunt and most of her guests and going on to the more fractious members of this present committee. I passed the postcard back down the line, collecting a censorious look from Beatrice Webb for not paying attention.

It was after ten o'clock when the meeting broke up. I wanted to catch the tram up to the top of Haverstock Hill, then clear my head with the walk home to Hampstead. I made for a side door. Shaw appeared from nowhere, one arm loaded with files and papers, and stuck the other across the doorway, cutting off escape.

'Assuming the intended victim to be a hard-working young woman anxious to play her part in improving society?'

'Then by all means prevent her from being murdered. Now if you'll excuse me . . .'

He smiled and angled himself across the door frame so that he was completely blocking it, long legs bent, beard jutting. I knew with a sinking heart that he'd argue for hours if necessary.

'Ah yes, but there are limits to my powers.'

It was the first time I'd heard him admit it. He still didn't look as if he meant it.

'Or rather, there are places where convention decrees I must not set foot. An actress's dressing room, for instance.'

'She's an actress then, this hard-working woman?'

'An inexperienced one. She's playing the lead in a little squib of mine, or will be if the Lord Chamberlain leaves any lines worth speaking.'

His last little squib had been a pro-suffragist one-acter that began with the Prime Minister having to disguise himself as a woman to get into Downing Street through rioting crowds. The censor had not been amused. I'd missed it, owing to being in prison again at the time, but my friends loved it.

'What's this one?'

6

'A pantomime.'

'I didn't think you liked pantomimes.'

'This one has a moral. Cinderella, five years after she's married her prince, deeply regretting it but trapped by our immoral divorce laws.'

'So who wants to murder your Cinderella?'

'Her husband.'

'In the play or in real life?'

'All too real.'

Something clicked.

'Might we, by any chance, be talking about Lady Penwardine?'

He smiled.

'She is acting under her own name of Isabella Flanagan. She prefers to be known as Bella.'

'She's left her husband and is having a love affair with Charles Courts.'

It was late and I was tired. Shaw, who can be something of a puritan, looked genuinely shocked.

'Nell, it isn't like you to listen to gossip.'

'I'm sorry. I was in bad company earlier this evening. I mean she's exerting her independence from an unfaithful husband.'

'That's better.'

'So does Charles Courts come into this at all?'

'Charles Courts is simply playing opposite her in my modest playlet.'

That surprised me. Courts, although a better than average actor, was what you might describe as a matinee idol, not the kind usually found in Shaw's plays.

'As Prince Charming. He hits off perfectly the manner of a man born to rule a wife and a country without understanding either of them.'

'Is that a description of Lord Penwardine too?'

'Lord Penwardine seems to think so. He's been trying every means available to have the play stopped, including threats.'

'Threats to his wife?'

'Yes. That's why we need your help.'

'I'm sure you're quite capable of dealing with any threats.'

7

Although in his fifties, he made a cult of physical fitness and was not above challenging people to box. As far as I knew, nobody had taken him up on it recently.

'I've far too much to do. Besides, it needs another woman.'

'I've far too much to do as well.'

He seemed to sag with disappointment. He let his back slide down the door frame and folded his legs like a stick insect until he was actually sitting down in the doorway, bearded chin on his rough tweed knees, looking up at me. His voice slid into a soft Irish brogue.

'Nell, in the name of good nature, in the name of common humanity, at least come and see this poor woman.'

I burst out laughing, I couldn't help it. I knew it was carefully calculated like all his seemingly impulsive moves, but it worked. It was easier to give in a little than to stay there arguing.

'When do you want me to see her?'

He was on his feet at once.

'Tomorrow, ten o'clock sharp, at the Crispin Theatre off the Strand. It's the dress rehearsal.'

I thought of all the other things I was supposed to be doing next morning but it was no use protesting. He was quite capable of folding up on me again. We parted outside the building and I walked to the tram stop. Once Shaw had gone I was angry with myself for giving in so easily.

TWO

THE CRISPIN IS A SMALL theatre wedged apologetically into a side street near Charing Cross station, a little removed from the main theatreland of the rest of the Strand. It alternated at the time between musical comedies and the occasional foray into the avant-garde works of Ibsen and Shaw without developing a public or identity of its own. At five-to-ten on a cold, grey morning, it had an unfestive look about it. The main doors onto William IV Street were locked and barred with old torn posters on either side. At least I thought they were old until I went closer and saw they were advertising George Bernard Shaw's latest one-act comedy, *Cinderella Revisited*, opening the following evening. The tearing had been done by the human hand rather than wind and weather, and they were smeared with tar. I couldn't imagine Lord Penwardine doing that himself, but perhaps he'd sent a footman.

I went round the corner into Chandos Place and found the stage door, set deep into sooty brickwork. It opened into a cavernous hallway with doors and pipes and staircases going off in all directions, and a pile of trunks and tea chests dumped in confusion as if by fleeing refugees. There was a porter's lodge with a sliding window to the right of the door, but it was unoccupied. I stamped, coughed and waited. Nobody came.

I called: 'Is anybody here?'

I could hear movement behind one of the doors. I called again, then a reluctant voice:

'Wait there. I'm coming.'

After some time a door opened and there was a plump, middle-aged man with a double chin and a paunch that

9

rounded out his black trousers and Tattersall check waistcoat. He looked buttery, from eating toast perhaps.

I said Mr Shaw was expecting me.

'They're all on stage.'

He sounded gloomy about it.

'How do I get there?'

He opened a door opposite and pointed down a long corridor, dimly lit by a few electric bulbs, with dingy green-painted walls and a line of doors on the right.

'Along here past the dressing rooms, turn right into the green room, left through there and you're backstage.'

I'd have been glad of a guide, but he wanted to get back to his toast. I went along the corridor into a room furnished with old but comfortable-looking armchairs and sofas. From there I could hear the murmur of voices. Along another, shorter corridor and I was in the wings, looking out from half darkness into a pool of light.

There were six people on stage. One of them was Bernard Shaw talking to a nondescript young man. From his worried and apologetic air, I assumed he was the producer. The other four, three men and a woman, were in costume. Shaw saw me almost at once and beckoned me over to join them. I went carefully, dazzled by the light.

'Here's Nell Bray come to watch over us. Nell, let me introduce the cast. This is our fairy godmother, Sylvia Bonnet.'

Sylvia was in her mid-forties. Under the heavy stage make-up with its upswept eyebrows and eyelids the colour of damsons, her face was strong and practical, her eyes watchful. She wasn't wearing a wig and her own dark hair had undisguised streaks of grey. Her costume was like a nurse's uniform with an incongruous starry cloak over it. Her handshake was cool and firm.

'Sylvia's husband Silvester is playing Buttons.'

'Enchanted.'

Silvester made a courtly bow. He looked a year or two older than his wife, with a head of silver-grey hair like a ship's bow wave and the air of a dissipated bishop. It went oddly with his maroon page's uniform and pillbox hat.

'This is Vincent Colvin. He's Dandini.'

Vincent was standing a little apart from the others. As Shaw had been introducing the Bonnets I'd been aware that he was looking at us in a quizzical way, trying to place me. He was in his early thirties, wearing court costume with knee breeches and buckled shoes. His hair was sleek and black, coming down in a peak over a high forehead. He wasn't conventionally good-looking, his nose too prominent, his eyes too deep set, but there was a nervy, intelligent air about him. He shook my hand and said he was pleased to meet me.

'And this is Prince Charming, otherwise known as Charles Courts.'

Shaw's voice changed when he introduced Charles, as if he found it a joke. Of the four, he was the only well-known actor. I'd seen his Romeo and Hamlet but never been nearer than the middle of the stalls. Now, as he smiled and put out his hand to me, my first feeling was one of annoyance. As if women didn't have enough problems without men as handsome as this being allowed to wander freely around the world. They should carry a warning bell, like lepers.

A quiff of brown hair fell over his forehead and his eyebrows had that little lift to them that makes a person look clever even if he isn't. In spite of heavy stage make-up he had a look of health and outdoors. He made you think of walks on a windy heath and tea by a roaring fire and . . . Warning bell.

'I'm delighted to meet you, Miss Bray.'

A smile that might have passed for shy. A voice that still carried with it the air of a rose-twined balcony on a summer night in Verona. Well, it was his job. He probably couldn't help it very much.

'And Mr Freeson, our producer.'

I'd been right about the nervous man. He gave me a strained smile.

If they were curious about what I was doing there none of them asked questions and Shaw turned to the business in hand.

'While we're awaiting the pleasure of Miss Flanagan and the Lord Chamberlain I suggest we begin the first scene.'

11

Silvester Bonnet and Vincent Colvin walked into the wings and Silvester came back on stage carrying a pair of boots and a boot brush. He and Freeson began discussing some piece of stage business while Shaw led Sylvia, Charles and myself down some side steps, across the orchestra pit and into the front of the stalls. As I settled down beside Shaw I asked him:

'Is there trouble with the Lord Chamberlain again?'

His struggles with that official – technically a member of the King's household but in reality the censor of plays – were already legendary. No play of his opened without long wranglings with the Lord Chamberlain's office about its morality, its politics or both.

'He promised to let us have his improvements on my unworthy words by dress rehearsal. We sent him a script two weeks ago.'

'And Lady Penwardine – I mean, Miss Flanagan?'

'She promised to be here at ten o'clock. We live in reasonable hope of seeing her by noon.'

There were quick footsteps in the wings. A woman came running onto the stage, coat flying, red hair falling down her back.

'Mr Shaw, everybody, I'm sorry, I'm sorry, I'm sorry.'

The accent was pure Boston. She came running to the footlights, dropping a mock curtsey on each 'sorry'.

Shaw sat there in silence, face expressionless, until she came to a halt.

'If only, Miss Flanagan, you could make an entrance in performance half as effectively as you do every time you're late, there might be some hope for you.'

She bowed her head, mock-humble.

'Nell, may I introduce to you Miss Bella Flanagan, the newest and incomparably most aggravating leading lady in London? Bella, this is Nell Bray. If you've been reading the newspapers she should need no introduction, except that she's twice as desperate a character as they make out. She's come to take care of you, against her better judgement, so you will do what she says.'

Bella Flanagan seemed not in the least put out by Shaw's introduction. She was perhaps four or five years younger than I was, in her late twenties, and several inches shorter. She wasn't conventionally pretty with her wide mouth and square jaw, but her hair was the colour of a winter sunset and she had a crackling vitality that gave the impression things would always be happening round her.

'And why have you kept us all waiting?'

'I had the last fitting for my costume for the balloon scene.'

'And you're quite satisfied with it?'

She ignored the sarcasm in Shaw's voice.

'Completely.'

'We're all very glad to hear it. So now, if you would oblige us by changing into your costume for your first scene, we may possibly even be able to start this rehearsal.'

She went. Ten minutes or so later, in green dress and jacket, she was there on cue for her first scene with Buttons. Cinderella complains to Buttons about the sad state of her marriage five years after meeting her prince. Buttons urges her to stay with her unsatisfactory husband on the grounds that under the present divorce laws she is better off being unhappily married than trying to make an independent life for herself. Cinderella, enraged, stamps three times and summons up her fairy godmother, blaming her for getting her into the trap in the first place.

Both the Bonnets, Sylvia and Silvester, were generous actors, doing what they could to help Bella. And Bella needed all the help they could give her. It wasn't that she lacked confidence. She spoke in a clear ringing voice like a clever student reciting the American Declaration of Independence, but there was a difference in kind between her and the two professionals. The next scene was a long dialogue between Charles Courts as the prince and Vincent Colvin as Dandini. They were both good but Colvin seemed to me the more impressive. His timing, the slightest movement of his head, conjured up the world-weary dandy to perfection.

After their scene we were back with Bella again. Cinderella, after a brisk talking to from her fairy godmother, confronts her husband to demand her freedom and the reform of the divorce laws. Bella,

13

explaining why the law was unfair to wives, really threw herself into it.

' "The slightest frailty, an hour's unfaithfulness on my part, and the law allows me to be cast off forever. But he, even if he's bedded every titled slut in Mayfair . . ." '

A rustling among the cast. A cough from Shaw.

'Miss Flanagan, if you refer to the words I, your humble playwright, happen in my fumbling ineptitude to have written, you'll find the line runs ". . . even if his immorality is the talk of society".'

'Yes, but that's what it means, isn't it?'

Shaw was dangerously courteous.

'Even my mild reference to immorality is likely to bring down on us the wrath of the Lord Chamberlain. Your version would probably close us down altogether.'

'And I used to think you had freedom of speech in England.'

'As I've tried to explain to you, if it exists anywhere it does not apply to the British stage and especially not to my plays. I shall be delighted, when we have a spare hour or two, to discuss the question further. But may we, as a personal favour and just for the present, get on with this scene?'

The last words came out as a suppressed shout. Even Bella looked alarmed and went through the next few minutes in a state of stunned obedience. But I noticed that, as the scene went on, she was moving gradually across the stage, closer to where Charles Courts was standing with a princely air by the property fireplace.

'Where do you think you're going, Miss Flanagan?'

Shaw sounded like a school teacher with a difficult ten year old.

'Across to Charles.'

'Well, you're not supposed to. Remind her what the stage direction says, please, William.'

Freeson read gloomily from his seat in the stalls: 'She stands by the window, one hand on the sill. He remains by the fireplace with the stance of a man defending hearth and home.'

'You hear, Bella? And you're gravitating towards him

14

like a besotted bride just home from her honeymoon. Over there with you, and please bear in mind that I don't write stage directions just to fill in blank spaces on the page.'

She went, not looking in the least abashed, with a glance at Charles that he was too professional to return.

Shaw said: 'We'll take it from Charles' dignity speech.'

Charles said: ' "You might at least have some respect for my dignity and your own." '

Bella came back with spirit: ' "Dignity! Where's the dignity in the office of gaoler?" '

Charles: ' "Gaoler?" '

Bella: ' "Worse than gaoler. At least a man who runs a common lock-up does it for society. You do it for nothing but your own self-importance against a woman you swore to love and honour." '

Charles: ' "And what about your vows to me?" '

Bella: ' "Vows! If you'd drugged me or made me drunk you couldn't have done me a worse wrong than to . . ." '

Shaw: 'Miss Flanagan.'

Shaw didn't even have to raise his voice. When really angry it had a cutting quality that would split slate. Bella stopped, half-way across the stage to Charles, and turned to Shaw with an air of polite inquiry. When he saw he had her attention he dropped his voice to that wheedling, exaggerated brogue that I knew as a danger sign, but Bella probably didn't.

'Would you be kind enough to inform us where you think you're going now?'

Bella said: 'I'm crossing from stage left to stage centre.'

'Are you indeed? Tell us, pray, with what object?'

'To get to Charles.'

'And what did you propose to do with Mr Courts when you got to him?'

A blush mounted from Charles' faultless collar to his firm jaw. Sylvia Bonnet, who wasn't needed in this scene and had come to sit beside me in the stalls, stirred in her seat and groaned quietly.

Bella explained from the stage: 'I thought it might be effective. You know this is where she says people shouldn't

15

be allowed to take binding vows while they're under the influence of love.'

'I have some vague memory of writing such a speech, yes.'

'I thought, when she reminds him of how much they once loved one another, she might touch his arm, just lightly, and he might look at her as if . . .'

She was interrupted by a loud groaning, a melodramatic clamour, no less. Shaw had buried his head in his folded arms and was rocking to and fro. Thinking he was ill I jumped up to help him, but Sylvia pulled at my skirt.

'Don't worry. It's all part of the pattern.'

Shaw stopped groaning and raised his head.

'Let this be a lesson to me on the paltry power of the written word. Here am I, devoting years of my otherwise tolerably useful life to writing plays in the doomed belief that they might, just might now and again in favourable conditions, insert in some receptive mind the germ of an idea. This morning, from Isabella Flanagan, I learn that I have utterly wasted my time. You must excuse me, ladies and gentlemen, a little emotion.'

He was thoroughly enjoying himself. After a pause for effect he turned back to Bella.

'What are they talking about in this scene?'

She seemed a little disconcerted.

'Well . . . I guess, the end of their marriage.'

'Yes. The love they had for each other is dead, quite dead. Their marriage is the corpse of it and they are discussing the state of that corpse like two doctors over a dissecting table.'

Beside me I felt Sylvia Bonnet shudder.

'Yes,' said Bella, serious now. 'Yes, I see that.'

'You would no more walk over and touch your husband's arm than you would touch a diseased liver or a putrefying lung. You understand that?'

'Yes. I'm sorry.'

I guessed Bella had stopped thinking about Charles and was remembering her own unsatisfactory husband.

'We'll take it from Charles' speech again. And try to remember that Cinderella is trying to escape from her present marriage, not preparing for her next one.'

16

This time the blush got as far as Charles' perfectly sculpted cheekbones.

THREE

SOON AFTER ONE O'CLOCK WE broke for lunch. We still hadn't got to the end of the play but this time it wasn't Bella's fault. A stage-hand announced to Freeson that they were still having trouble with the balloon and Shaw seized on this to give the cast a chance to rest and eat. As he rushed out he called up to Bella on the stage:

'Now you're to do exactly what Nell tells you.'

It looked as if he expected me to start my body-guarding duties at once but Bella seemed occupied with Charles. They were there alone on the stage, heads close together. She looked downcast and I wondered if he was reading her a lecture on professional behaviour. I went up the steps from the orchestra pit and across the stage, giving them plenty of time to hear me coming. She turned. Her smile seemed genuine.

'Miss Bray, I'd wanted to meet you even before this. Will you have lunch with me?'

Certainly, I said. Charles was apparently not included in the invitation because he smiled and strolled away into the wings.

He said, over his shoulder: 'You will be careful, won't you?'

'Of course. Miss Bray's looking after me and we'll take a hansom. No dark doorways.'

Her eyes followed him for a moment, then she turned to me again. 'Can you wait while I change? I won't be long.'

The sun had come out while we were in rehearsal and we picked up a hansom without trouble outside Charing Cross station. As we went up Haymarket she asked me what I thought of the play.

'It's clever. Of course it's much the same case against the divorce laws as he makes in *Getting Married*. Did you see that?'

'Twice. That's what made me write to him and ask him to write a play for me.'

Light began to dawn.

'You mean, you commissioned the play yourself?'

'I tried to, only he wouldn't take any money for it. He said I couldn't afford him. He did it because he felt sorry for me.'

More likely, I thought, because it was another chance to give a good stir to the social beehive. All very well, but when you did that you never knew who'd end up being stung.

We came to Berkeley Square with its leafless plane trees and the austere houses of the rich rearing up all round us. The hansom slowed down and came to a halt. Bella bit her lip.

'I hate to ask this, but would you mind getting out first and seeing if there are two men looking as if they're waiting for somebody?'

I got down and had a good look round. A Victoria with a chestnut mare waited outside one house, a motor car with a uniformed chauffeur outside another. A Fortnum's delivery van was driving away from the other side of the square. Apart from that, nothing. It was not an area that encouraged loafers.

'Nothing I can see.'

She got down, paid the driver and led the way up some steps to a front door newly painted in geranium red. The door opened apparently of its own accord as soon as her foot touched the top step and revealed a butler waiting inside.

'Good afternoon, madam.'

Our coats and hats transferred themselves into his hands.

'Thank you, Peters. Will you please ask Naomi to bring lunch for two to my study?'

I followed her up a staircase spread with gold-coloured carpet, like thick honey, past a mirror in an ornate frame that looked like Grinling Gibbons and probably was. On the first landing Bella opened a door into a room decorated in shades of violets and greys, long, silver curtains looped back from windows overlooking the square, three sofas piled with big, bright cushions. The elegance was relieved by a plain wooden desk in the far corner overflowing with letters and pamphlets, and a bookcase stuffed with legal books and, as far as I could see, everything ever published by George Bernard Shaw. She gestured towards the sofa.

'Make yourself comfortable. May I call you Nell? Lunch will be here soon.'

I sat down in an armchair by the fire.

'Does your husband want to murder you?'

She settled on a sofa opposite me and tucked her feet up, careless of the marks made by her muddy shoes.

'Yes, if he can't stop me any other way.'

'Stop you doing what exactly? Leaving him?'

'No. In his circle wives are leaving their husbands all the time, but ever so discreetly. He has the country house, she has the town house and they meet once a year for the tenants' Christmas party. You know the kind of thing.'

'Not at first hand.'

'What Guggles is worried about isn't that I've left him but I'm trying to divorce him and making him look ridiculous.'

'Guggles being . . .?'

'The Sixth Marquess of Penwardine, George Unwin Gregory Glaston-Vass. My lawful wedded husband, heaven help me. I tell you, Nell, when I have anything to do with making laws it will be a criminal offence for any woman to get married under the age of twenty-five.'

A knock on the door. A plump maid pushed in a trolley loaded with plates and covered dishes, and began laying them out on a table near the fire. Bella went on talking.

'You take a girl with some spirit, some ambition and what does she do? She throws all of it away on the first man who speaks seriously to her.'

'Were you very young when you married Gug . . . Lord Penwardine?'

20

'Twenty-two. Old enough to know better, but my mother and father had both been killed in an accident the year before. You've probably heard of him. Firebrake Flanagan they called him. He invented a new braking system and insisted on going down the steepest gradient he could find in a rail car behind his private locomotive, my mother along with him, to prove it worked. It didn't. Pa would never be told. I take after him.'

'Will that be all, madam?'

The maid had finished putting out the lunch. There were two kinds of bread rolls, three kinds of cold meat, smoked trout, a shapely bottle in an ice bucket.

'Yes thank you, Naomi, that will be all.'

As she wheeled the trolley out its wheels left tracks in the thick carpet. Bella caught my eye.

'I can't break them off madam.'

'Have you tried very hard?'

She looked at me sideways.

'You're shocked?'

'Curious. You commission plays from Bernard Shaw and you drink champagne at lunchtime.'

'Everybody should drink champagne at lunchtime. The trouble is, the people it would do most good for are the ones who never get it.'

She ignored the champagne flutes the maid had left on the table and collected two pewter mugs from the top of the bookcase, giving them a quick rub with the penwiper from her desk.

'It tastes better out of these.'

She popped the cork expertly and poured about half a pint of champagne into each mug.

'Confusion to Guggles.'

I decided I could drink to that. We sat down at the table and helped ourselves to trout.

'As I was saying, I was twenty-two when I married him. It was my first trip to Europe. I'd come over for a friend's wedding. She was marrying a Scottish earl and I met Guggles at the reception and fell head over heels in love with him. I could have no more been stopped than they could stop Pa getting into that rail car. All right, I know

21

what you're thinking.'

'I was thinking that champagne does taste better out of a pewter mug.'

'You're thinking that I fell in love with him because of his title and because he was quite handsome in an English sort of way. I wasn't that green, not even at twenty-two. No, I married Guggles out of a deep ignorance of the British constitutional system.'

She took a gulp of champagne and topped up our tankards, emptying the bottle.

'I suppose I'd been taught too much history and not enough politics. I thought English peers still carried on like they did back in the days of the Magna Carta. You see, I'd always planned to marry the kind of man who could change things.'

'And Lord Penwardine didn't live up to that?'

'He did not. The idea was that with his position and my father's money we could put right some of the things that needed putting right in England and show the rest of the world how to do it. So I married him and settled two million dollars of my father's money on him.'

I was beginning to know what the passengers must have felt like behind her father's failed braking system.

'You thought Lord Penwardine was a social reformer?'

'I knew he was a Liberal. I didn't know much about English politics at the time, so I guess I might have overrated that.'

'Quite possibly.'

'And then, three years after we're married, he calmly announces one day when we've got twenty-two people in for a quiet little dinner that he's going to be a Conservative. Apparently his family had been Conservatives from way back, but when I first met him they'd all joined the Liberal party because they were annoyed at some cousin or other not being made an ambassador. Can you believe that?'

'All too easily.'

'I called him a turncoat and walked out.'

'Good.'

'The trouble was, I was so blazing mad I'd forgotten that

22

when the hostess walks out all the other women get up and walk out with her. And would you believe that's just what they did, right in the middle of dessert? There I was, out on the terrace just wanting to get Guggles on his own and quietly strangle him, and eleven English ladies in formal dress trailed after me, wondering what they were supposed to do next.'

I started laughing. I wasn't used to champagne at lunchtime, or to Bella. She joined in and Naomi, coming to collect the remains of lunch, found us shaking with laughter over an empty bottle.

'Shall I bring the coffee, madam?'

When we'd both recovered I said: 'So that was when you realised he wasn't going to reform the world?'

'Oh, I knew that by then. All he'd managed to reform was the roof of the ancestral home, a few hundred acres of shooting and a hound pack. All on my money.'

'So you left him?'

'Yes. This year was the last straw, with the politics and a few other things. But I can't get rid of him.'

I sipped my coffee and wondered about those few other things. If they included Charles Courts, that was the rub. Under the totally unfair divorce laws, Lord Penwardine could divorce his wife if he could prove she was committing adultery. But sauce for the goose wasn't sauce for the philanderer. He could have as many affairs as he liked, but they wouldn't constitute grounds for divorce unless Bella could prove what the lawyers called 'aggravated adultery'. Desertion by the husband could aggravate adultery and so could cruelty, but joining the Conservative party wasn't likely to come under that heading.

I looked round the room, at the rich curtains, the carved and gilded mantelpiece, the portrait by Boldini of Bella in evening dress.

'Still, at least you've been able to take your money away with you.'

The sparkle died out of Bella. She looked grim.

'Oh no I haven't. All this is from my mother's bit of money and that's running out.'

23

'What? Under the Married Women's Property Act, you have a right to take your own property on separation.'

'Oh, I know all about that.' She gestured to the books by her desk. 'But that doesn't affect a settlement freely entered into. When I married Guggles I put my father's money into a trust fund for the Penwardine family. I suppose we thought there'd be children and . . .'

Her voice trailed away.

'So you can't get your money back if you do manage to divorce him?'

She smiled, an odd, strained smile.

'Oh, my lawyers weren't totally incompetent. If I divorce him for cruelty or desertion I can take it back. But what chance have I got of that with your divorce laws stacked against me the way they are?'

'And if he were to divorce you for adultery?'

Tactful or not, I had to ask it. She didn't take offence.

'In that case, he keeps it, every cent. Only he's not going to do that.'

'So what it comes to is that you're trying to force your husband to let you divorce him?'

'Yes. It's only fair. He's been in love with another woman since before he married me. I caught him writing letters to her when we were on our honeymoon, poor girl.'

She said it with sadness rather than anger.

'But why did he marry you?'

'For my father's money, of course. I don't suppose he'd have thought of it himself. His mother talked him into it. The Dowager Marchioness, that's Lady Dorothea. She probably persuaded him it was his duty to the family.'

'And you want him to admit his adultery with this other woman and . . .'

I was going to say '. . . and provide proof of cruelty against you'. Under our mad divorce laws it has been known for erring husbands to pretend to beat their wives, before suitably primed witnesses, to give them the proof that brought legal release for both of them.

'Oh no. I wouldn't want him to do that to the poor woman. I've done her enough wrong without meaning to. I don't want to hurt her any more. She can have him with

24

my blessing.'

'But how . . . ?'

She leaned towards me.

'It's so simple. He's had other affairs. All he has to do is provide evidence of adultery with some other woman whose reputation doesn't matter, then pretend to hit me in front of witnesses. Then he can marry this woman he's wanted to marry all along and I can have my freedom and my father's money and . . .'

'And marry Charles Courts?'

She gave me a long look.

'Yes, and marry Charles Courts. That's why I want my father's money back.'

'Is he that expensive?'

I couldn't have blamed her if she'd resented that. I was trying too hard not to be over-impressed with the man. Luckily, she didn't seem to be annoyed at plain speaking.

'Oh, Charles isn't expensive at all, but aeroplanes are.'

'It seems an odd hobby for an actor.'

'It's not a hobby, Nell, it's the future. Aeroplanes are to this century what my father's railroads were to the last one. He'd want me to do this with his money. And Charles is more a flier than an actor. He'd give up acting tomorrow if he could.'

Her eyes were bright, her whole body vibrant with enthusiasm. I was beginning to see how she'd bowled over Shaw. It was only a few months since Bleriot had flown his machine across the Channel and a lot of otherwise sensible people were going down to air madness as to 'flu. Still, no woman had yet been divorced for being unfaithful with a flying machine, so this wasn't the point.

'Are you having a love affair with Charles Courts?'

She looked at me levelly.

'If you mean have we made love together, the answer's no. My husband can keep an army of spies if he likes, but he can't prove Charles and I have been in the same bed, because we haven't. And we're not going to until I've divorced Guggles.'

I felt sorry for them, which given her money and his looks was not reasonable.

25

I came back to our starting point.

'And you think your husband wants to murder you?'

'Yes. That way he could marry the other woman, keep Father's money and stop being made to look ridiculous. In the circumstances, wouldn't you want to murder me?'

'Has he made threats?'

'He sent me a letter when the news about this play first got out. He said if I appeared in it I'd regret it and he'd take any necessary steps to stop me.'

'Has he done anything so far?'

'He tried to get an injunction in court, but it was thrown out. Then one day after we started rehearsals somebody got in and tried to burn some scenery.'

'You think your husband did that?'

I found it hard to imagine the Lord Penwardine I'd met doing anything so practical.

'You don't light fires yourself. You get the servants to do it for you.'

'You think he sent a housemaid?'

'Some of his hunting friends would do any dirty work for him – Piggy Ditchbrake and the rest.'

'Anything else?'

'Two men tried to attack me as I was coming out of the stage door two nights ago. I think they were trying to kidnap me. I screamed and hit out, and luckily Charles was just coming out, so they ran off.'

'Did you recognise them?'

'No. It was dark.'

'So they might just have been men trying to snatch your bag?'

'I don't think they were. They were trying to drag me away.'

'Did you tell the police?'

'It wouldn't have done any good. Guggles has friends everywhere. Look at what's happening with the Lord Chamberlain.'

I was beginning to see that Bella related everything to her own predicament.

'Bernard Shaw has had trouble with the censor before, you know.'

26

'But why is it taking so long? Here we are at dress rehearsal and we still don't know what he's going to do with the script. I'm sure that's because of me and Guggles. I wouldn't be surprised if he's got a spy in the cast, listening to everything that goes on at rehearsals.'

'Have you told Bernard Shaw that?'

'No, It might upset him.'

'You couldn't do that with a cavalry charge.'

The butler came in with letters on a tray. There were about a dozen of them and she began flicking through them without much interest. As he went out she asked him to call a cab to go back to the theatre. Then she gave a little gasp that might either have been fear or annoyance.

'From him.'

She held out to me a square envelope of thick, creamy paper with a crest on the back.

'Lord Penwardine?'

She nodded and opened it. There was just one small sheet of paper inside. She read it at a glance and passed it to me. There was no kind of salutation, just five lines:

If you persist in this undignified exhibition tomorrow night I give you final warning that the consequence will be your responsibility and not mine.

Penwardine.

'What do you think he'll do?'

'I don't know what he means to do, but he can burn in hell as far as I'm concerned.'

She threw the letter onto the fire and held it there with the poker as it twisted, charred and finally burst into flames. When it was no more than a skin of black ash, she looked at me and smiled.

'Shall we be getting back to the dress rehearsal?'

FOUR

BELLA'S DRESSING ROOM WAS BLEAK: a chair facing a mirror with an electric light over it, a second chair with a padded seat but hard wooden arms, a rail for clothes and a tall cupboard. The only touch of luxury came from two large boxes with the name of a well-known couturier blazoned on them and two hat boxes. A gaunt woman in a black dress was standing beside them, her arms full of soft blue leather and grey fur.

'Ma'am, there are two of them. Have they made a mistake?'

'No, I ordered two. Nell, this is Mercy Phipps. She's the wardrobe mistress and she's kindly helping me dress.'

Mercy gave me a glance and persisted: 'But why two?'

'I get hot in that last scene, Mercy. I sweat. This play goes on for six nights. Can you imagine what it would be like by the end of the week with just one outfit?'

Mercy looked at me and raised her eyebrows. She wasn't used to this concern for personal hygiene among her actors, or the budget that could gratify it.

'Besides,' said Bella, 'it's my flying-away suit, my aeroplane outfit. I can wear it when Charles takes me up as a passenger.'

Even Mercy couldn't help laughing. Although at that time only a handful of women had flown as aeroplane passengers, the newspaper fashion writers were already taxing their brains with what the well-dressed woman should wear in the air.

I asked: 'What's Cinderella doing with an aeroplane outfit?'

'It's the end of the play. I fly up and away in a balloon to

28

freedom and a new life.' She raised her arms. 'I wanted an aeroplane but Mr Shaw said it wouldn't fit backstage, so we'd have to make do with a balloon. Still, I think we've got the costume right. Help me on with it, Mercy.'

It was an amazing costume, a kind of ankle-length leather tunic in a sky shade that Bella assured me was called 'aviation blue'. The skirt was divided so that it could be tucked into the top of long, silver leather boots, giving the effect of trousers. Turned-back lapels were faced with grey chinchilla fur and a matching fur scarf cascaded down from a kind of blue leather turban to twine round Bella's slim neck. Between the fur and leather her eyes sparkled, and her mouth broke into a great smile.

'Do you like it, Nell? Will it do for a going-away costume?'

I guessed that she was thinking of more than the play. Publicly flying away from her husband was the event for which she'd had the costumes designed. A rough and nervy business, and yet it shouldn't be allowed to smell of sweat. I was beginning to see that as typical of Bella Flanagan.

As Mercy was fussing over the scarf, Sylvia Bonnet put her head round the door.

'Mercy, could you help me with my cloak?'

'I'll help,' I said.

Bella was safe in Mercy's hands and after our lunchtime conversation I wanted to know more about the rest of the cast. Sylvia's dressing room was like Bella's, but more homely. There was a bag of russet apples on the table among the sticks of greasepaint, a wooden monkey on a string hanging over the mirror. Dressing rooms were life for Sylvia, not a staging post in a matrimonial battle. Or so I thought until she remarked in a purely conversational tone:

'I'm going to skin Silvester alive.'

'What's he done?'

'He promised me faithfully he'd stay out of public houses at lunchtime, and where is he? Drinking over the road, that's where.'

She flapped her starry cloak and showed me how it

needed pinning at the waist to make it hang properly. Given Shaw's teetotal views I could understand her worry.

'Have you both worked with Bernard Shaw before?'

'Oh yes.'

'What did you mean this morning when you said it was all part of the pattern?'

'When he was tearing into Lady Bella? He falls in love with his leading lady, writes a part for her the way he wants her to be in real life, then gets angry with her when she isn't.'

'Bernard Shaw in love with Lady Penwardine?'

I found it hard to reconcile with the man I knew. Sylvia gave me a sideways look.

'Oh, no impropriety. No funny business. It's all words with him, which is just as well in the circumstances.'

'Meaning?'

'Well, you saw for yourself this morning, didn't you? If her husband wants grounds for divorce, he wouldn't need to do much more than send a spy along to rehearsals.'

This surprised me, chiming as it did with Bella's idea of a spy in the cast. I pinned the spangled net, being careful not to skewer Sylvia.

'Do I get the impression you don't care for Bella?'

'Oh, I like her as a person. There are no airs about her and give her her due, she works hard. But amateurs have got no business on the real stage and I don't like the way she's using us. It will lead to trouble and I don't need any more of that, not with Silvester.'

The door opened. Sure of his welcome, rosy-faced and smiling, Silvester walked in. I could smell the whisky fumes as he kissed her. She pulled away.

'I'm not talking to you. You promised.'

'I had to see a man about a dog. Don't be angry, love. It was only one little drink.'

He beamed at me and slid an arm round her waist. She pulled away.

'I'm supposed to be on stage and so are you. Go away and change.'

He stopped at the door and blew us a kiss. She pretended not to see.

'Shall we go?'

Bella was waiting for us outside in the corridor, magnificent in her blue and silver with the blue turban hiding her hair. We went together to the stage where Charles and Vincent were in costume and waiting, but there was no sign of Shaw or the producer. Charles came over to join Bella and they began talking in low voices. I saw him glance towards me and guessed she was telling him about our conversation at lunchtime. Vincent sat on his own, long stockinged calves outstretched. He was humming to himself an odd, jaunty little tune.

There was a stir in the wings. Bernard Shaw appeared, beard jutting, hands behind him. He had the air of a man bringing important tidings. Behind him, looking smug but embarrassed, came someone I hadn't seen before. He was a nondescript man of about thirty, very small and a little round-shouldered, clean-shaven apart from a lick of dark moustache. His trousers were pinstriped, his boots black and highly polished. His round spectacles reflected the stage lights so that he looked like a drab insect with bright, multi-faceted eyes. Behind him trailed Freeson, looking even more worried than usual.

'Ladies and gentlemen.'

Shaw's voice promised revelations. Bella and Charles broke off their conversation. Vincent stopped humming. Silvester, who'd come running in from the wings opposite still doing up his page's costume, skidded to a halt.

'Ladies and gentlemen, may I present to you the Lord Chamberlain?'

The nondescript man wiggled his moustache in the beginnings of a protest.

'Or rather, I should say, the Lord Chamberlain made flesh in the person of his representative here on earth. May I introduce to you Mr Matthew Migson, assistant deputy chief clerk to the Examiner of Plays?'

He said it like a herald announcing a chivalric title. The moustache wiggled again, but this time it looked pleased, like a rabbit's nose meeting a succulent lettuce leaf.

'We are singularly honoured because for the first time, as far as I know, in modern theatrical history, Mr Migson

31

is to join our company.'

'What?'

The protest came from Charles.

'At the Lord Chamberlain's expense, I hasten to add. Apparently I and my small play are considered so dangerous to the order of society that it is not enough for the Lord Chamberlain to convey his instructions by letter. Mr Migson has brought them here in person and, what's more, Mr Migson will be here with us for every performance to make sure that these instructions are carried out. Is that right, Mr Migson?'

Migson cleared his throat.

'Er, substantially the situation is much as you present it, Mr Shaw.'

He seemed unaffected either by Shaw's irony or the experience of being centre-stage. His voice was deep for his size, plush with self-satisfaction.

Bella had been staring, wide-eyed. Now she found her voice.

'They're not allowed to do that, are they?'

'Apparently they are.'

'It's because of me, isn't it? Because of my husband. It's his friends again.'

It struck me that it might be because somebody in the Lord Chamberlain's office had heard of Bella's habit of altering her dialogue as she went along. But in that case, who had told him about it?

Charles said to Shaw: 'Surely you aren't going to allow this?' He was tense with anger.

'If the Lord Chamberlain chooses to use public money to give one of his staff the inestimable benefit of attending my play six times over, I can hardly object.'

'It's an insult to all of us. Do we have to stand for it?' Charles sounded unexpectedly pompous. Migson didn't help matters by catching his eye and giving him a self-deprecating little smile.

'The alternative would seem to be to cancel my play.'

Charles gave a shrug that seemed to say that would be a price worth paying.

Bella said angrily: 'No. That would mean my husband

had won.'

Charles looked at her, seemed to be on the verge of saying something, but didn't. In any case, Shaw had already come to his decision. He made a deliberately elaborate business of getting Migson comfortably settled in a chair on stage, then took a stand beside him, holding several pages of typescript.

'These are the changes that the Lord Chamberlain has been pleased to ordain, fifty-three in all. So if you'll kindly find your scripts. Page three, line four, delete: "Half the English aristocracy are unfaithful to their wives . . ." Insert: "Even some titled people are said to be unfaithful." '

Shaw's voice was deadpan but his formidable eyebrows rose and fell like guillotines.

'Line five, delete: ". . . and the other half are incapable".'

A cry of protest from Bella, silenced by a glance from Shaw.

'Bottom of page, delete: "His long gallery is full of three centuries of slaughtered stags and portraits of unhappy wives." Substitute: "His long gallery is full of sporting trophies." '

'It's obvious who's behind this.'

'Page four, line four, delete . . .'

And on we went, through all fifty-three of the changes. Bella simmered and muttered, scoring angrily at her script with a gold propelling pencil. Migson was attentive throughout, occasionally crossing and recrossing his pin-stripped legs, looking like an artist pleased with his work. At long last they got through the list and could start the dress rehearsal of the last scenes.

The arrival of Migson had put Bella into such a bad temper that she fairly scorched through the final scenes. She flung her accusations and her claim for freedom at Prince Charming as if he were her husband in earnest. Charles, by contrast, was as near wooden as an experienced actor could be, resentment in every line of his body. Apart from having to refer to their scripts now and again to take in the Lord Chamberlain's changes, the play went to its final moments without interruption.

Cinderella tells her prince to go and learn to be a motor

mechanic and her fairy godmother summons up a balloon to waft her off to her new life as a free woman. The balloon was a deliberately comic affair made of painted canvas with a real woven cane basket underneath and a banner slung across it: 'The Independent Glass Slipper Co'. Sylvia stamped on the boards. A canvas screen with a cupboard painted on it was hoisted quickly into the flies, revealing the balloon on stage behind it. Bella fired her last line at Charles:

' "Then perhaps you'll be more use to the world than you were to me." '

As she spoke, Silvester was crossing the stage with a small set of steps, putting them in place beside the basket. The sides of it were lower than an ordinary balloon basket, so that Bella would stay visible to the audience for her short flight. She went lightly up the steps, sat on the edge of the basket with her ankles crossed to shake hands with Buttons, then swung her legs inside, lithe as a gymnast. Three stamps from Sylvia were the signal for the men on the ropes to raise the balloon while another began to close the curtains so that the audience's last sight would be Cinderella waving from the basket, flying up and away.

But before the curtains could close or the balloon rise more than a few feet there were shouts of 'Look out!' from the stage-hands. The balloon came down again and the curtains stopped where they were. The problem was Migson. He'd suddenly left his seat near Shaw and myself in the front stalls and, before anybody thought to stop him, clambered through the orchestra pit and up the steps to the stage. If the stage-hands hadn't seen him in time he'd have been knocked off his feet by the closing curtains. He was standing there at the front of the stage shouting something that we couldn't hear at first above the comments of the stage-hands.

'. . . must discuss . . . must look more closely . . . wearing trousers.'

When we eventually got Migson and the stage-hands calmed down it turned out that his complaint was that Bella was outraging public decency by wearing trousers and, worse still, flaunting them as she climbed into the basket. Bella looked incredulous, Vincent amused. Charles sighed heavily and turned his back on Migson. But Shaw had a glint in his eye and I could see he intended to use the incident in yet another attack on the inanities of censorship.

'Bella, shameless woman, the Lord Chamberlain's representative objects to your wearing trousers.'

She played up to him, perching herself again on the edge of the basket.

'But they're not trousers, Mr Shaw. It's a divided skirt. Look.'

With Migson gazing at her like a fish in an aquarium, she unbuttoned the top of a silver boot and untucked the leather tunic. A little kick sent it flying into the air, revealing a knee in a blue striped stocking. The kick was in Migson's direction. He walked closer until he was only a few feet away from her, chest heaving from his anger. The rest of us, even Shaw, watched fascinated to see what he'd do next. For those few moments Migson held the stage as completely as any actor who'd ever graced it. Bella watched him, the smile freezing on her face.

When he took another step I thought for a moment that he was going to attack her. Charles, who had turned round, thought so too, and I saw him go tense and begin to move. Another step and a little gasp from Bella. Migson had actually laid his hands on her, or at least on the soft leather skirt she'd flaunted at him. From where I was standing I could see the expression on his face and it seemed to me one of transcendental smugness. A cat tasting salmon might look like that, or a connoisseur sipping a legendary wine.

Bella tried to pull away from him, kicked out, missed him and fell backwards into the basket. Charles crossed the stage in a couple of strides and, with a straight-armed sweep, delivered a blow to Migson's cheek that must have been audible at the back of the dress circle. Migson stood there, hand to his cheek. In spite of the blow the look of satisfaction hadn't entirely faded from his face. Charles looked at him for a moment, then stalked away into the wings. It was left to Cinderella's fairy godmother to help her out of the basket. While she did it, Shaw and I led Migson out of harm's way.

FIVE

SHAW LEFT IT TO ME to show him out of the theatre. By then his smugness was back in place and he showed a tendency to linger. As we went along the corridor to the stage door he said:

'Are those the dressing rooms?'

'That's right.'

I hurried him along, but not before he'd heard Bella's voice floating out from behind a closed door.

'. . . and then that awful little man put his hand . . .'

I assumed she was telling Mercy Phipps all about it. Migson's moustache twitched, but apart from that he gave no sign that he'd heard.

The stage door-keeper was showing out a small party. They looked like a mother and two daughters up from the country, pink-faced and inclined to giggle. When he saw me and Migson he was obviously in a hurry to get rid of them and practically pushed them through the door. Migson followed more decorously. As the door closed behind them the door-keeper gave a me a look that mingled guilt and appeal. Although I couldn't see that trio presenting any danger to Bella, I was curious.

'Sightseers?'

His hand was in his pocket, jiggling coins.

'There's no harm in it. You wouldn't tell Mr Shaw or Mr Freeson?'

'Not if there's no harm in it, but what exactly is going on?'

'Mr Courts, miss.'

It took me a while to make the connection.

'You've been letting people in to dress rehearsal to see

Charles Courts?'

'The women.' He said that as if it were some kind of excuse.

'The things some of them would do to get a look at him you wouldn't believe. There's a friend of mine who works at the theatre where he did Romeo, he had this quite elderly woman – he said she was forty-five if she was a day – offering him a thousand pounds if he'd let her hide in his dressing room.'

'And did he?'

He looked censorious.

'Of course he didn't. More than his job was worth. Then there was this other one who kept turning up in a wedding dress, flowers, veil, the lot, saying Mr Courts had promised to marry her. Had to call the police to her in the end.'

'How many of them did you let in this afternoon?'

Two things were on my mind. One was that they'd have seen more of their hero in action than they expected and unless Bella and Charles were very lucky the gossip would be all round London. The other was that with a door-keeper as bribable as this one, Bella's husband could send in a squadron of kidnappers if that was what he had in mind.

'Only the three boxes, and I tell them they have to keep quiet and sit well back. There were the ladies you saw, then a couple of younger ones and an old one on her own.'

'How much?'

He swallowed.

'Two quid a time or five pounds for the three.'

Which made eleven pounds he'd picked up that afternoon alone, easily three times his week's wage. I hadn't realised Charles was such an industry.

'You won't tell Mr Shaw?'

The door-keeper's eyes were moist and anxious. He really hadn't meant any harm.

'I won't tell him. Only you will be careful, won't you? You know there might be trouble at the opening night tomorrow.'

'Oh yes, miss. Nobody will get past me tomorrow. Besides, all the boxes are booked. Full house tomorrow.'

I supposed I'd have to be content with that and was thinking of going back to the dressing room to see Bella when the stage door opened and a young woman came in, glancing around nervously. She saw me first and gave a little start.

'Oh. Oh, I'm sorry. Do you work here?'

Her voice had a little lisp to it. She was quite small, no more than five foot two with fair hair and a soft look that went with the voice. She was wearing a cream-coloured dress, a brown coat with a narrow border of mink, more mink on the cuffs of her brown leather gloves. Fluffy tendrils of hair escaped from beneath a fur hat, framing an anxious little face with big grey eyes. Her mouth was rosebud-shaped but reminded me more of a finch's beak. It had a hungry, thrust-forward look that didn't match the softness of the rest of her. I said I was just visiting and gestured towards the door-keeper. She turned to him.

'I . . . I wanted an address.'

He glanced at me with an I-told-you-so look.

'And whose address would you be wanting, miss?'

'Mr Courts'.'

Her face went pink.

'I . . . I just wanted to know where he lives. To send him a letter to tell him . . . how much I admire his acting.'

It came out in a series of little gasps. She was scared but determined. Goodness knows how long she'd spent screwing herself up to this. I felt angry with Charles, as if it were his fault.

'You address letters to the theatre, miss.'

'It's . . . it's not the same. Not personal.'

Silvester Bonnet strolled past in outdoor clothes, raised his eyebrows at me and went out. The door-keeper lifted the counter of his glass booth and shut himself inside it. He became very formal.

'Any letters for members of the cast should be addressed care of the stage door. They will be conveyed to them at the first suitable opportunity.'

I wondered if this sudden respect for the rules was because I was there as a witness.

The blonde woman stood without saying anything, as if

hoping he'd change his mind. Then she turned to me. There was something like desperation in her voice.

'Have you seen the play?'

I nodded.

'Does he ... does he play love scenes with Lady Penwardine?'

I laughed. Faced with this desperate determination over such a question, I couldn't help it. Before I could apologise a door opened along the corridor and we heard Bella's voice, loud and clear.

'Goodnight, Mercy. Goodnight, Sylvia. See you tomorrow.'

The blonde woman gasped and fled.

If she'd waited she'd have had her chance to see Charles face to face, but I doubt whether she'd have enjoyed it because he and Bella came walking along the corridor together, deep in conversation. I said to Charles:

'An admirer of yours has just gone out.'

He looked alarmed.

'Not the woman in the wedding dress?'

'Not yet, but heading that way by the sound of it.'

'Damn. I'd better go out by the front door. I'll meet you there.'

Bella said firmly: 'Don't worry, Nell's going to see me safely home, aren't you, Nell?'

'I'd be happier if I came with you too.'

'No. It's better if we're not seen leaving together. I'm sure that awful little Migson will still be hanging round. I'll see you tomorrow afternoon.'

I went out first and there was a pause before Bella followed me that would have given time for a kiss or a hand squeeze, not that it was any business of mine.

As we walked round the corner into William IV Street I noticed the blonde woman some distance away on the other side of the road. She saw us at once, quickly turned her back and hurried off in the opposite direction. I decided not to draw Bella's attention to her. It was bad enough that a woman could be so silly, without advertising the fact any more. We came into the Strand, where people were queuing under the lighted canopies of other

40

theatres. Twenty-five hours from now and, for better or for worse, the curtain would be going up on the first performance of *Cinderella Revisited*.

'I feel nervous, Nell. Is that silly?'

'Perfectly normal, I'd have thought. Even professionals must be nervous about first nights.'

'Not just that. About Guggles. You saw his letter.'

'Do you think he intends to do anything tonight?'

'I don't know, Nell. I just don't know.'

We turned towards the station to pick up a hansom cab.

After a few more steps: 'Would you come and stay with me, Nell? Just for tonight.'

I didn't fancy a night in the oppressive luxury of Berkeley Square, and anyway the cats would need feeding.

'Why don't you come and stay with me instead? I don't suppose he'd think of looking for you up in Hampstead.'

Her face lit up.

'Could I, Nell?'

We went to Berkeley Square first to collect her toothbrush and a change of underwear. We left with two suitcases and a hatbox but she said that was because her maid would insist on wrapping everything up in tissue paper.

The hansom was waiting outside and I told the driver to take us back to Charing Cross.

'But I thought we were going . . .'

I pushed her inside.

'There's not much point if everybody knows where we're going.'

'But there was nobody there but Naomi and the butler. I'm sure they wouldn't . . .'

'Probably not, but we're going to take this seriously.'

It was still half in my mind that she was playing games, that all of this was no more than a scheme to force her husband into the kind of public desperate act that would give her the grounds for divorce. If so, that game shouldn't be played entirely on her terms.

At Charing Cross we unloaded the two cases and the hatbox and carried them down in the lift to our new electric underground railway. It was the pride and joy of

41

Hampstead and Golders Green, this line only two years old carrying us smoothly home from our work in the centre of town. Bella had never been on it before and knew enough about railways to be impressed. She even volunteered that she'd insisted on having electricity installed in Guggles' ancestral home before she moved in after the honeymoon, to give some of the family ghosts notice to quit.

'Only I quit and they stayed.'

From Hampstead station we walked up to my narrow home on the top of the hill. No electricity there and as cold as chapel because I'd been out all day, but Bella was like a child with a new doll's house. She stood on the little landing while I shifted piles of papers out of the spare room so that she could move in.

'What are they all?'

'That pile is the minutes of the Women's Social and Political Union, the other is notes on the Poor Law Commission. The one under your hatbox is a petition to the Home Office on prison conditions.'

She followed me downstairs and watched while I put a match to the fire and filled the kettle. I turned one of the cats out of the basket chair by the fire so that she could sit down.

'Do you do this kind of thing all the time?'

'Acting as a bodyguard?'

'No, politics.'

'As much of the time as I can manage. Now and then I take on some translation work from French or German to earn some money.'

'And that's what you live on?'

'Not entirely. My father left me some shares that bring in a hundred and fifty pounds a year. I decided helping to get the vote for women was my main work.'

She looked at the flames licking their way round the kindling and sighed.

'Guggles and I were going to travel the country together, looking at slums and schools, deciding what had to be done.'

Her voice was less hard than on the other occasions when she'd mentioned him.

'But he wasn't interested?'

'Oh, he thought he was for a while. I could probably have kept him interested if it hadn't been for his mother going on about his duties to his family and his duties to his class and his duties to his tenants. It was a battle for him between that woman and me, and she won.'

I'd have thought Bella would have been a match for most women, but I remembered Lord Penwardine's mother as I'd seen her at my aunt's reception and understood.

'That woman thinks we're still living in feudal times. As far as she's concerned we are. You should see them at home, Nell. Tenants touching caps and schoolgirls curtseying. Curtseying, I ask you. At least I stopped them doing it to me. That was one of my two petty triumphs there.'

'What was the other?'

'The food cart. This you won't believe. Every mealtime the servants bring in metal containers and we scrape what's left of our meal into them to be sent out to the grateful peasantry on the estate. All right, sometimes there'll be most of a ham or a joint of beef or something, so I suppose it might do some good. But would you believe what she did with it?'

The kettle boiled. I made tea.

'She scraped it all together into those containers, beef and cold potatoes and custard all in together. What's the point of that? The only point was to keep them in their place, to let them know that they might get free food but it had to be disgusting. Can you imagine?'

I said I could. She sounded genuinely distressed.

'That was one thing I managed to change. One container for meat, another for vegetables, another for dessert. And I tell you, Nell, that woman used to watch me as if she thought I was leading the next French Revolution.'

I noticed that she didn't mention what must have been the greater cause of friction, the pressure on her to produce a son. I made us toasted cheese for supper and opened a bottle of decent sherry I'd been keeping for Christmas. After that she settled down by the fire to learn

43

the changes the Lord Chamberlain had made to the script and I got out my Remington and caught up with some of my mail. Around midnight we settled down in the basket chairs, each with a cat on her lap, and rewarded ourselves with another glass of sherry.

'You know, Nell, this is the kind of life I'd like. Being useful.'

She asked what I was grinning at. I told her about the door-keeper's activities and the women who were desperate for a look at Charles. I impressed on her that she shouldn't tell Bernard Shaw about it, but I wanted to see how she'd react.

She said: 'It's ironic.'

'Ironic?'

'They all want him for his looks. Nell, I promise you, I shouldn't care if he looked like the hunchback of Notre Dame. It's that when I'm with him I feel there's a future, that there's a big world out there and we're part of it, not stuck on some feudal reservation doing the things people did five hundred years ago.'

The fire was burning low. Just before we got up to go to bed she said in a subdued voice:

'Do you think he'll be in trouble for what happened today?'

'Hitting a man from the Lord Chamberlain's office? Oh, twenty years in the Tower at least.'

'Seriously?'

'Seriously, I suppose it will depend on whether Migson decides to make an issue of it. We must hope it won't come to anything.'

'Nell, I'm worried about tomorrow.'

She had a lot to be worried about and most of it was her own doing but I refrained from pointing that out. I saw her up to bed, then settled down at the table to get on with some of the things I should have been doing had Shaw not inveigled me into this.

SIX

BELLA SLEPT LATE THE NEXT morning and I kept her up in Hampstead and out of harm's way until after lunch. At about four o'clock I delivered her to her dressing room, where Mercy Phipps was already putting out her two changes of costume, green day dress for the first scenes, the blue and silver ballooning costume and leather turban for the end. There was a huge arrangement of roses and carnations in a silver basket standing against the wall. Bella gasped and ran over to it. Mercy said, without looking up:

'Mr Courts brought them. He said somebody had sent them to him and he didn't want them, so he thought you might as well have them.'

I thought it was just as well that one of Charles' rich admirers would never know what became of her tribute.

With Bella settled I decided to go over to Holborn to collect some books I needed. She seemed alarmed.

'You'll be back for the performance?'

I promised. Outside it was already dark. The lights had been switched on under the theatre canopy and fresh posters replacing the vandalised ones advertised the first night. A few rough-looking characters were idling round, but that was nothing new in the Strand. I went on my errand to Holborn, was delayed a little and hurried back with my books under my arm at around seven-thirty, with just an hour to go to curtain rise.

I was crossing the Strand opposite the turning for William IV Street when I saw somebody I recognised crossing from the opposite direction. He was in a hurry, striding across the road without paying much attention to the traffic, wrapped in a black coat with a bowler hat pulled down over his high forehead. There was enough light from the vehicle headlamps for me to be quite sure of his identity. A hansom just missed him and the driver swore but he didn't appear to notice. The likes of Lord Penwardine don't bandy insults with cab drivers.

When I recognised him I wished I'd stayed with Bella. I made a move towards him, then had to jump back when an electric tram burped its horn at me. Sneaky vehicles. At least with the horse trams you get more warning. By the time the tram had gone past he was on the opposite pavement, striding in the direction of Trafalgar Square so purposefully that the theatre-going crowd streaming in the other direction made way for him. There was no point in running after him and the sensible thing was to go to the Crispin and find out if he'd been causing trouble. I continued my journey to the opposite pavement and turned the corner to find a riot in progress.

It was quite a small riot. At first, from the sprinkling of glossy top hats and good black overcoats among it, I thought it was nothing more than an excited first-night crowd. But there were very few women and a buzz was rising from it that, from half-way down the street, I knew meant trouble. It was a puzzling crowd, perhaps a quarter of it in top hats or bowlers, the rest in flat caps. It was milling round as if waiting for something without knowing what it was waiting for. As I watched, an overripe orange squashed against a *Cinderella* poster. A few cheered. A top-hatted one blew a hunting horn. The police, as usual when they might have been useful, were nowhere to be seen. Voices sounding far from sober set up a chant:

'Come out. Come out. Come out.'

I went on down the street and spoke to a very tall top-hatted man leaning against a lamp-post on the fringe of the crowd.

'What's happening?'

It took him a long time to focus on me. When he spoke it was clear why he needed the lamp-post.

'Itsh a protesh.'

'Protest against what?'

'Aboush people breaking up marriages, making

46

husbands laughing stocksh.'

'What people?'

'A vicksen little vixous . . .' He tried again. 'Vicious little vixen we've got holed up inside there. Haven't we, Piggy?'

The man who'd blown the hunting horn had appeared beside us. He was short and plump, his face glistening.

'Have to send for the terriers.'

He blew another blast on his horn.

One of the cloth caps yelled from the crowd: 'Hey guvnor, don't you talk to her. She's one of them. She's carrying books.'

From the way he said the word I might as well have been carrying typhoid. The hunting horn sounded again, right in my ear. I knocked it out of Piggy's hand. The crowd set up a noise half-way between a yell and a jeer. In trouble again, and really not my fault.

For once, help appeared when I needed it.

'This lady is a friend of mine.'

An overcoated arm hooked itself through mine. A fume of whisky wafted across my face.

'Good evening, Mr Bonnet.'

The plump man looked taken aback. He began to protest.

'It's nothing to do with you. She was interfering . . .'

Silvester Bonnet gave him a warning look and shook his head. The plump man subsided.

'Good evening to you, dear lady. Shall we take a walk together?'

Silvester, quite deliberately, was implying that we were rather close friends. He knew his audience. The jeering gave way to cat-calls and laughter.

'How very kind.'

I moved off with him as smoothly as possible towards the street corner and the safety of the stage door. The plump man was searching the pavement for his hunting horn. I managed to kick it into the gutter as we went but he got no sympathy. The crowd was temporarily on Silvester Bonnet's side. A ribald chorus followed us.

We got to the stage door, the crowd trailing a few yards behind us. It was shut but the door-keeper must have been watching through a peephole because it opened just long enough to let us in, then slammed shut against our followers. The door-keeper was breathing heavily and looked sick with fear.

'Are the police out there yet?'

'No sign of them.'

He dived back into his cubbyhole. I thanked Silvester for the rescue.

'A pleasure. It was nothing compared to the Birkenhead Argyle on a wet Monday night. A classical training's all very well, but there's nothing like the halls for knowing how to deal with a crowd.'

Freeson, the producer, came rushing along the corridor, looking both scared and angry.

'Silvester, where have you been? The curtain's up in forty minutes.'

'Don't worry, my dear boy. I could make up as King Lear in three minutes flat, not to speak of Buttons.'

He winked at me and ambled off towards the dressing rooms. Freeson turned his anxiety on me.

'What's happening out there? If the police don't come soon the audience won't be able to get in.'

'They want to get at Bella. Is she all right?'

'She's still in her dressing room. We haven't told her what's going on.'

'Somebody will have to tell her.'

The shouts and cat-calls from outside were suddenly louder. Freeson winced.

'And Mr Shaw's not here yet.'

'I think that might be him arriving now.'

I looked out through the peephole but all I could see were the backs of the crowd on the corner of the street. Then there was a sight I never expected to be pleased to see, a file of policemen pounding past in a blur of navy blue. A whistle shrilled.

'Thank God for that.'

The policemen were followed by the sound of cantering hooves, either the arrest vehicle or somebody had called the fire brigade for good measure. I saw a police truncheon land on broad shoulders, the crowd scattering

48

from the corner. Then a group of policemen came running back in our direction, hustling a familiar red-bearded figure. Freeson joined me at the peephole.

'They're arresting Mr Shaw.'

'No, I think they're rescuing him.'

I pulled the door open and Bernard Shaw and three policemen fell through in a contentious knot.

'I asked you to let me speak to them. Am I not even allowed to address a few words to Englishmen outside a London theatre?'

'Now sir, you know it would only cause more trouble. You're much better off inside.'

The sergeant was doing his best to be conciliatory.

'The state employs you as the citizen's protector, sergeant, not his nanny.'

'Fortunately, sir. Anyway, I don't think you'd find many outside to speak to now. We've persuaded them to move on.'

The hooves rattled back along the side street, probably bearing a few of the more obvious trouble-makers to the police station. I hoped Piggy and his hunting horn were inside, but doubted it.

Freeson said to the sergeant: 'Can the audience get in now?'

'Yes, sir. I'll leave two of my men on duty to see you're not troubled any more.'

The door-keeper, reassured at the sight of blue uniforms, opened the door to let them out. Bernard Shaw was trying to cheer up his producer.

'Rioting in the streets before they've even heard a word of it – what more can you want?'

He asked if the cast were all there and Freeson, still shaken, said they were. I was glad he didn't mention how narrowly Silvester had made it.

'And Miss Flanagan?'

I said: 'I'm going to see her now. It's only fair to warn her.'

'Wish her luck from me.'

As I went along the dressing-room corridor, I thought she'd need that, and more.

SEVEN

BELLA WAS SITTING ON HER own in front of the mirror, fully dressed and made up for her first entrance, reading from her script file. She looked pinched with nerves.

'Where have you been, Nell?'

'There's been a touch of trouble outside. It seems to be over now.'

'My husband's friends?'

'Yes, I think so. There was a tall drunk one and a fat one called Piggy.'

'I knew he'd be there. Did I tell you he's . . .?'

She'd been fiddling with a stick of greasepaint. She dropped it and bent to pick it up.

'He's what?'

'Like Guggles' spaniel. There's nothing he wouldn't do for him.'

And yet I had the impression that wasn't what she'd intended to say before she dropped the greasepaint.

'Was Guggles there?'

There seemed no point in lying. I told her I'd seen him crossing the Strand. It looked to me as if he'd stayed long enough to see the riot started, then slipped away before it could lead to embarrassment for him.

'He's not going to stop me, Nell. They can burn the theatre down and we'll perform in the ashes, but he's not going to stop me.'

I agreed with her. Even if Bella was responsible for some of her own troubles, she was a better cause than the likes of Piggy Ditchbrake.

She asked me to hear her lines. I didn't think there was much to be gained at the last minute, but at least it was a

50

distraction. We hadn't got through more than a page or two when there was a knock on Sylvia's door, then on Bella's.

'Five minutes, ladies. Five minutes, please.'

Sylvia looked round the door, calm and reassuring in her nurse-cum-fairy godmother costume. Now that Bella had company I could go and find the seat that was being kept for me in the front row of the stalls. Freeson had warned me that Migson would be sitting beside me. Perhaps the idea was that I should restrain him if he showed signs of leaping up on stage and laying hands on Bella again. All in all, I wasn't looking forward to the performance. I met Silvester in the corridor, sauntering towards the stage in his Buttons costume, apparently without a care in the world. He directed me through the green room to a small corridor that led to the front of the house.

I found my seat just before the lights dimmed, in time to see Shaw sitting in the middle of the row, beard propped on his steepled fingers, face intent. The seat on my left was empty and there was no sign of Migson. I glanced round the rest of the audience and saw there were more men in evening dress than you'd expect for a Shaw first night. After what I'd seen outside that wasn't a good sign. Nor was the presence at the front of the gallery of a group of men who looked as if they'd come straight from their market stalls.

The lights went down. The curtains drew apart to reveal Buttons on stage, polishing boots.

Buttons, to audience: ' "Have you ever noticed, the less a man does, the more boots he needs to do it in?" '

Laughter. Silvester held them effortlessly through his monologue and Vincent Colvin entered as Dandini with just the right air of condescension from courtier to servant in discussing the prince's domestic problems. His exit was the signal for Bella's first entrance.

There was a round of applause as she came on. She looked alarmed for an instant, then couldn't keep back a smile. In expecting trouble from her husband's friends I'd forgotten that she'd have her own supporters in the

51

audience. The combined appeal of rebellion and aristocracy had brought her a lot of goodwill. Buoyed on that warm tide she went through the first scene swimmingly, much better than I'd expected. The opposition, if I was right about its presence, hadn't uttered a sound.

It was a short play with no interval planned, so the lights in the auditorium stayed down while furniture was shifted for the second scene. The scenery – the prince's kitchens – would stay the same throughout except for the final scene, when the cupboard would rise to reveal Cinderella's balloon ready on the stage behind it.

The first sign of trouble from the audience came near the start of the second scene, in the dialogue between Cinderella and her fairy godmother. Sylvia got a laugh on her line about most wives' managing very well in spite of their husbands but it didn't seem to me an entirely friendly laugh. There was a prolonged bray from a few rows behind me which sounded like the sort of noise Piggy Ditchbrake might make. I saw Shaw turn round to look. Then there was an outbreak of applause and foot stamping, and a few ragged cheers breaking out from various parts of the circle and gallery. Cinderella's husband had entered and some of the house seemed to think he needed support. Charles was too experienced to be thrown by it. He asked Cinderella why her trunks were packed. She replied it was because she was going to leave him.

' "But you are my wife." '
' "Is that a life sentence?" '
'It is for him.'

The cry, unscripted, came from the front of the circle. A few people tittered, some shushed. Up in the gallery somebody squeezed a hooter that made a loud belching noise. On stage the warring husband and wife gave each other a glance of desperate complicity and ploughed on.

' "You married me of your own free will." '
' "A silly girl married you. Now she's grown up." '
Piggy's voice yelled: 'Into a silly woman.'

More laughter, but angry voices were raised from the

stalls. A loud bang from the gallery as somebody let off a firecracker. Piggy, judging his moment, stood up and blew a blast on his hunting horn. A male usher came running down the aisle, bent on eviction. More burps from the hooter and blasts of firecrackers. In the gallery a fight had broken out. On stage Charles raised his voice and fed Bella her next line. There wasn't long to the end of the scene. Against a background of mounting noise from the audience that meant she and Charles had to bellow their lines at each other like town criers, she made it to her exit speech and swept out, head high. Vincent, entering from the other side for his short dialogue with Charles, met the wave of sound and launched himself on it, but with practically no chance of being heard. The opposition was drunk on its own success, so that even the absence of Bella made no difference. When it came to Charles' exit they gave him what was probably meant to be a sympathetic cheer. Vincent and Silvester between them had the task of closing the scene against a chorus of yells and hooting and several more firecrackers. Whether they'd actually reached the last line before a relieved stage-hand let the curtains swing together, only they would know.

The curtains stayed together for the next half hour or so during the skirmishing to eject Piggy Ditchbrake and the rest. The house lights came up, then almost immediately went out again and for a minute or two we were all in confused and bad-tempered darkness. We found out later that somebody in the circle had torn an electric cable away from the wall and it was only by good luck the whole theatre didn't catch fire. Luckily the old gas lights had been left all over the theatre when electricity was installed and some of the staff had the sense to light them. When they did come on, their soft yellow glow revealed general confusion.

Two ushers were closing in on Piggy Ditchbrake, who was standing on his seat and flailing about him with his dented hunting horn. The stage door-keeper appeared from a side door, gave one horrified glance, then screwed up his courage and went to help them. Both circle and gallery had their own battles going without visible intervention from theatre staff. Bernard Shaw was standing in the centre aisle of the stalls holding by the collar a very drunk young man who seemed to be trying to bite him. Seeing a couple of men in evening dress advancing on him from behind I ran up the side aisle to make a diversionary attack on them. Subsequent proceedings were neither dignified nor scientific but they ended with the carnivorous young man and the other two in retreat. Shaw dusted his hands off and shouted to me above the noise:

'Now for the one with the horn.'

By this time the ushers and the door-keeper had dragged Piggy into the aisle, but he'd managed to escape from them. He stood there, very red in the face, still blowing his horn. Whether he expected his hound pack to come surging to his rescue, goodness knows. Shaw grabbed him by one arm, I by the other. In the comparative quiet after the horn I heard Freeson's voice floating pathetically out of the orchestra pit.

'Ladies and gentlemen, I beg you, ladies and gentlemen . . .'

As if in answer, what sounded like a louder firecracker went off. I'm sure, looking back, that the sound came from behind the curtain, but at the time that didn't register. There was still a lot of noise coming from the gallery and our hands were full. Shaw and I began to tow Piggy towards a side door, with an usher pushing from behind.

'Over here, sir.'

The door-keeper had the side exit open. We pushed Piggy through it and out into the cold night air, yelping like a trampled lap dog. The door-keeper shot the bolt with the air of a job well done.

'That's got rid of the worst one, sir. They might calm down now.'

EIGHT

THE DOOR-KEEPER WAS RIGHT, but it took another ten minutes before the stragglers were rounded up and the fights in circle and gallery subdued. As comparative calm settled I had time to think about Bella again and looked for the door-keeper. He was leaning against the back of a seat, panting and sweating.

'Is there anybody on duty at the stage door?'

He gave me an injured look.

'I can't be in two places at once, can I? When one of the stage-hands came and told me all hell was let loose out front, I thought I'd better come and give a hand.'

'Yes, but shouldn't you be back there now, in case any of them try and get in again by the stage door?'

He went slowly. By then two police constables had arrived and were completing the calming effect, although they seemed disposed to blame Shaw for everything.

'I suppose you'll be calling off the rest of it, sir?'

'Certainly not. I'd no more defraud my public by presenting two-thirds of a play than you'd let a publican serve you two-thirds of a pint of beer.'

'The electricity's gone off.'

'Then if necessary we shall do it by gaslight. Where's Mr Freeson?'

There was no sign of him. I guessed he'd gone backstage and volunteered to look for him.

'Tell everybody we'll be starting again in ten minutes. Meanwhile, I shall do my poor best to keep the audience entertained.'

In ejecting Piggy, Shaw had taken possession of his hunting horn. He carried it on stage with him and, standing in front of the curtains, blew a blast on it to claim the attention of a bewildered and restless audience. It sounded like a Valkyrie with laryngitis but it worked and within a few minutes he was holding them as only Shaw could, talking about his play and the scenes they'd just witnessed. As usual the Lord Chamberlain came in for ridicule and I wondered if Migson could hear, wherever he was. It was then about twenty minutes since the curtain had come down, ten minutes or so since I'd heard the firecracker from behind it.

I went backstage by the corridor Silvester had shown me. Several stage-hands were moving around in the dim light, two of them trying to work the old-fashioned stage lighting that probably hadn't been used for a decade. I found Freeson behind a flat representing one of the kitchen walls. He seemed to be looking for something.

'What is it?'

'You heard that firecracker, from up here on the stage? It could be smouldering. It could start a fire.'

The great horror in a theatre. He was shaking with nerves and anger.

'The stage-hands didn't see anybody?'

'No. There was nobody here at the time. But you can smell it, can't you?'

There did seem to be a faint whiff of firework in the air, but the gas lighting was making its own smells. A burst of laughter from the other side of the curtain seemed only to add to Freeson's worries.

'What's happening out there?'

'Shaw's making a speech to them.'

'Oh God.'

He sounded as if that were the final disaster. I delivered the message about starting in ten minutes and that made it even worse. But at that point, to ragged cheers from both sides of the curtain, the electric lights came back on. As if galvanised by them, Freeson abandoned his search for the firecracker and began giving instructions to the stage-hands. I decided my place was with Bella and went from backstage to the green room.

As I opened the door I heard somebody inside.

I called: 'Bella?'

I'd no special reason to think it was her, but she was the one on my mind. As I spoke, and before I could see inside the room, I heard the door opposite open and close and heavy steps walking rapidly away. A man's steps, certainly not Bella's. It added to the uneasiness I was feeling. I ran across the room and opened the door onto the short corridor. Nobody. Nobody, either, when I rounded the corner into the long dressing-room corridor. Whoever it was could have disappeared into any of the dressing rooms on my left.

I hurried on and tapped on Bella's door. Mercy Phipps' voice, sounding very strained, asked who was there. When I gave my name Bella called to me to come in.

'Will somebody please tell me what's happening out there? Are we starting?'

Mercy was helping her into the blue flying suit. Her eyes were bright, dangerously excited.

'Yes. Piggy Ditchbrake and the others have been thrown out. Are you all right to go on?'

'Of course I'm all right.'

Her fingers fumbled at the buttons until Mercy took over. I thought she must have been more than half convinced that the play would be abandoned, otherwise she'd have changed her costume some time ago. I guessed she was more scared than she'd admit.

'You heard how that man Piggy picked up on my dialogue? They all knew what was coming. Doesn't that prove what I said to you about Guggles having a spy?'

'Perhaps he thought of it on the spur of the moment.'

'Piggy Ditchbrake couldn't think of "Good morning" on the spur of the moment.'

Now that I knew she was safe I went back to the auditorium to find the audience still enjoying the unexpected bonus of Shaw's performance. A few minutes after I got to my seat Freeson popped his head out of the wings to hiss at Shaw in what was meant to be a discreet way that they were ready to start the final scenes. Shaw immediately broke off in mid-sentence.

'Ladies and gentlemen, I'm sorry to have to deny you

the pleasure of listening to me any longer. Let the play continue.'

Our throwing-out squad had done its work thoroughly. The play rolled along with no interruptions except the welcome ones of laughter and the occasional gasp at a line that had escaped the censor. The final confrontation between Cinderella and Prince Charming went off particularly well, because Bella was in such a state of anger that she hurled her lines at Charles like stones from a sling.

The last entrance of Sylvia as fairy godmother meant there were only a few minutes to go to the end of the play. I began to relax. On cue, as Sylvia stamped once on the stage, the canvas screen was whipped up to reveal the balloon with its basket and defiant banner. There was laughter, a scattering of applause. A final word from Cinderella to the prince:

' "Then perhaps you'll be more use to the world than you were to me." '

Bella turned away from Charles with a whisk of her chinchilla scarf. Silvester came bustling across the stage with the steps. The seat beside me was still empty and I thought it odd that Migson hadn't appeared. The steps were put in place. All that was left was for Bella to climb into the balloon basket and Sylvia to give the three stamps that were the signal for it to be drawn up towards the flies, carrying her away to freedom and independence. Bella's foot was on the bottom step. Every line of her body showed how much she was enjoying the climax of this public revenge on her husband.

When I glanced round everybody I could see was smiling. Bella might not be an actress, but she seemed to have the gift of carrying an audience with her. But of course most of the people left would be much of the same cast of mind, good Shavians with all the right opinions on the woman question. We were all willing Cinderella up and away in her bright balloon and her sky-blue costume. Buttons spoke his final line to the prince about marrying above your station. Charles, stage front, was managing to hold an expression of hurt and outrage in profile without looking ridiculous. The fairy godmother was smiling and waving; the curtains were beginning to quiver.

Another step. The applause was already swelling. Then it went wrong. With her foot on the last step Bella froze. Silvester, realising that something was amiss, moved towards her. Charles couldn't keep a shade of anxiety off his face. I wondered if this might be a last-minute production ploy to screw up the tension, but one glance at the way Shaw was sitting forward in his seat disposed of that idea.

The applause trailed away. Cinderella gave a choking cry and stumbled back down the steps, pushing Buttons aside. With a wild look on her face she came hurtling back across the stage into the arms of Prince Charming and buried her head in his chest, shoulders heaving. His arms automatically went round her but his face registered the shock of somebody faced with entirely unprofessional behaviour. That was our last view of them as the curtains swept together, leaving a few of the audience applauding but most of them looking questioningly at each other. Then there was a cry of 'Boo' from the circle, cries of 'Shame' from the stalls, tentative at first but strengthening as they found company.

At first I thought Lord Penwardine's claque had found its way in again, but these protests had another more familiar tone. They were the indignation of advanced, right-thinking people who'd unexpectedly had their beliefs trampled on by somebody they thought they could trust. They'd been given Cinderella flying away to independence, then, at the very last minute, she'd thought better of it and rushed back to the protecting arms of her unsatisfactory husband. I couldn't blame them for booing.

Shaw was already on his feet with a knot of people around him, arguing, gesticulating. He shook himself free of them with less than his usual politeness.

'Nell, come backstage with me at once.'

That was what I meant to do, but I didn't like the look in his eyes.

'Why?'

'Because I intend to strangle Lady Penwardine. I expect you to help me.'

I couldn't blame him either. I went.

NINE

'SHE WAS IN THE BALLOON basket. In the balloon basket in my flying outfit.'

We were in a pool of stage lighting, behind the curtain and within the topless cavern of backstage. On the other side of the curtain the audience had stopped booing but there was still a hum of talk and questions with the raised voices of the ushers inviting people to leave, assuring them that the play really was over. Bella was sitting on the sofa that formed part of the set, Sylvia on one side with an arm round her shoulders, Shaw on the other, awkwardly patting her hand and looking up at her with an expression of confused and, for once, speechless sadness. No talk now of strangling her. As soon as we'd arrived on stage we could see that something had gone badly wrong. Bella had been standing there, clinging to Sylvia, who was trying to stop her seeing what the men were doing around the balloon basket.

Now Charles, Vincent and Silvester, along with Freeson the producer, were standing in a knot around something that was lying close to the basket on the boards of the stage. Charles and Vincent had lit cigarettes. Charles tried to wave me away as I went over to them, but there was no point in that. They'd covered the body with Sylvia's fairy-godmother cloak. Bella's leather and fur turban lay beside it.

'What happened?'

Silvester's make-up was smeared. He looked sick but very sober.

'Shot.'

'Who is she?'

There was a silence, an awkward silence. Again it was Silver who answered.

'It's not a she.'

'Who is it?'

'The Lord Chamberlain's man. Migson.'

'What was he doing in Bella's costume?'

A stage-hand came running from the wings. 'There's a policeman outside. He's on his way.'

I knelt down and pulled the cloak back. Migson's eyes were open, the mouth with its rim of red lipstick slightly open too. His cheeks were powdered, eyebrows shaped into half moons with black wax pencil. The back and sides of the soft leather tunic were so thoroughly soaked with blood that it had begun to spread across the front. Kneeling down I could see that blood must have splashed over Charles and Vincent when they lifted him out of the basket. The white silk stockings of their court costumes were spotted with red.

'What happened?'

Either Charles or Vincent said: 'Shot in the back.'

The policeman turned out to be a young and very worried constable, clearly not used to sudden death. Shaw had recovered enough to take an interest in what was happening and suggested that he should send for a senior officer, so the stage-hand was sent running again. Other stage-hands were watching from the wings and the dimly lit space at the back. It seemed an instinct with them to leave the stage space itself to the actors, even in this emergency. Shaw went back to Bella and the constable stayed, looking almost as disconcerted by the actors in their costumes and make-up as the body at their feet. When he brought himself to look at Migson's face he said:

'I suppose he was one of the actors too.'

The others left the explaining to me.

'No. His name was Matthew Migson. He worked for the Lord Chamberlain's department.'

The constable looked even more unhappy.

'What exactly happened to him?'

I left that to one of the others. After all, they'd been on stage.

Charles said reluctantly: 'We don't know what happened to him. All we know is that the actress playing the lead saw him in the basket when she was about to step into it at the end of the play.'

'Dead?'

'Of course he was dead. He was lying crumpled up in the basket with her hat on top of him.'

'You should have left him there for us to see, sir.'

Vincent Colvin said: 'Supposing he'd been alive and unconscious? He'd have needed treatment. We couldn't just leave him there.'

The constable glanced across at Bella.

'I'll need to speak to the lady who found him.'

Charles said quickly: 'Is that necessary at present? She's had a bad shock and couldn't tell you anything we haven't.'

'She's Lady Penwardine, isn't she, the one there was all the trouble about?'

Charles made an impatient noise.

I said: 'She acts under her own name of Bella Flanagan.'

'And that's Bernard Shaw sitting next to her?'

'Yes, it's his play.'

He thought weightily for a moment.

'Mr Shaw doesn't like the Lord Chamberlain's department very much, does he?'

I had visions of the country's leading playwright being dragged off in handcuffs. To put a stop to it I said: 'That doesn't mean he'd murder one of his staff. Besides Mr Shaw was only a few feet away from me when Migson was probably shot, down in the audience with several hundred witnesses.'

The constable pounced.

'How do you know when he was shot?'

'I think I heard it. At the time I thought it was just somebody letting off another firecracker, but looking back I think it came from behind the curtain.'

Freeson said, 'I heard it too.'

At the time he'd been appealing for calm from the orchestra pit, much closer to the stage than I was.

'Didn't you do anything about it, sir?'

'I went backstage to see what was going on.'

The constable was beginning to look interested. 'And what was going on, sir?'

'Nothing. Nothing but the smell. I thought it was a firework, but it must have been . . . must have been the shot.'

'And nobody? No stage-hands?'

'Not then. They'd all gone to try and find the old lighting gear. They came back just after I arrived.'

'Did you go straight backstage, sir, after you heard what you thought was a firework?'

'Yes . . . that is, no, not quite.' Freeson looked the picture of guilt and misery, but then he usually did. 'You see, there were fights going on in the auditorium and there were people attacking Mr Shaw and . . . I didn't know what to do. I waited for a few minutes, I suppose, then I didn't seem to be doing any good out there and it struck me there might be a fire risk, so . . .'

'So how long would it be, sir, between hearing it and going backstage?'

Freeson gazed despairingly round at us, as if we might have the answer.

'Four minutes, five minutes. I don't know.'

'And did you look in the basket, sir?'

'No. I had no reason to look in the basket. Why would anybody let off a firework in a basket?'

I left them to it and went over to the sofa. Bella disengaged a hand from Sylvia and held it out to me.

'Oh Nell, what am I to do?'

'You'll have to talk to the police, I'm afraid. There should be somebody more senior on his way.'

I don't think that was the answer she wanted but her question struck me as odd in the circumstances.

'They say . . . it was Migson.'

'Yes.'

'Shot?'

'Yes.'

'Why was he wearing my costume?'

'I don't know.'

We sat there wordlessly, Shaw on one side of her, Sylvia on the other, myself kneeling on the floor, holding her hand. She kept glancing towards Charles. That was the state of affairs when Inspector Merit arrived, bringing a sergeant and several more constables with him.

He was a plump and balding man with protuberant brown eyes who, from the start, insisted on addressing Bella as Lady Penwardine. He herded us all with lugubrious politeness into the green room, then, presumably when he'd viewed the body, came to apologise for keeping us. He said he'd need to talk to us one by one, starting with Lady Penwardine. Bella stood up. I could tell she was trying to look composed but there was fear in her face as well as misery. The ballooning costume that had looked so jaunty on stage seemed odd and sinister now. The inspector held the door open for her and she went slowly past him and out. Charles' eyes never left her, but this time she didn't look at him.

The inspector stationed another constable in the green room to keep an eye on us. He sat on a chair by the door with his legs stretched out giving Bernard Shaw an occasional jaundiced look as if he expected him to jump up and do something outrageous. He needn't have worried because I'd never seen Shaw look so subdued. I went to sit beside him.

'Poor Bella, he should let her go home.'

'I'm sure he will, once he's taken a statement from her.'

'What can she tell him?'

'What can any of us tell him? I assume you didn't see Migson walking around in Cinderella costume?'

He shook his head.

At first there was some quiet talking as people compared notes, but it soon died away and we sat trying not to stare at each other. All the cast were there, plus Freeson. I assumed that the stage-hands and other staff had been gathered in another room. Charles sat on his own with his arms folded and his eyes fixed on the floor. Sylvia and Silvester huddled together, looking tired. At one point he even managed to drop off to sleep, his head lolling against her shoulder, but woke himself with his first snore. Freeson fidgeted and Vincent Colvin sat with his legs crossed, smoking cigarette after cigarette.

After half an hour or so the sergeant reappeared and asked Shaw to go with him. I assumed that meant the inspector had finished with Bella. I wondered whether I should go to her, but thought the inspector had probably given orders that we should all wait where we were until questioned and I didn't want to start an unnecessary fight. As it turned out there wouldn't have been time. Shaw had been gone no more than ten minutes before the sergeant came back.

'Miss Bray, would you come and see the inspector now, please?'

He'd taken over a small room behind the box office and was sitting at a desk in front of wooden pigeon holes stacked with different-coloured tickets. He half stood up when I came in and invited me to take the seat in front of the desk. The sergeant settled himself into a corner with a notebook as the inspector gave me a long look.

'I've seen you before somewhere, haven't I?'

'Probably in court.'

'Yes.' He sighed deeply.

With his prominent eyes and bald dome he looked like a large, patient frog. His voice had a slight Hampshire burr to it. I found myself disliking him less than I usually disliked policemen and warned myself to be careful, although I wasn't yet sure of what.

'Would you be kind enough to tell me, Miss Bray, what you were doing here tonight?'

I'd had plenty of time to anticipate this and had decided there was no reason to lie. I explained about Shaw's appeal to me and my reluctant role as guardian of Bella. He heaved another sigh when I had to touch on her battle with her husband.

'I've heard from Lady Penwardine and Mr Shaw that there was a certain amount of . . .' – he hesitated – '. . . of opposition during the performance.'

'Some allies of Lord Penwardine tried to sabotage it, yes.'

'What makes you think there was any connection with him?'

'I know one of them was a friend of his, called Piggy

65

Ditchbrake. I first saw Piggy making trouble outside the theatre an hour before the performance began. A few minutes before that I saw Lord Penwardine himself crossing the Strand.'

He raised his eyebrows, increasing the frog effect.

'So you didn't see Lord Penwardine himself at the theatre?'

'No, but I don't know what else he'd be doing in this part of London.'

He sighed again. I noticed that the sergeant had stopped taking notes and wondered if he'd been given a signal.

'I'm afraid we seem to be getting away from the matter in hand, Miss Bray. I gather from the constable that you think you heard a shot.'

'Yes. Without realising what it was at the time.'

'What time would this have been?'

I'd been thinking about that too.

'You've heard they had to bring down the curtain because of trouble in the audience? I should say it was probably ten minutes or so after that, but a lot was going on and I didn't check my watch.'

The sergeant was taking notes again.

'Did you know the deceased, Mr Migson?'

'I first set eyes on him at dress rehearsal yesterday.'

'Did you see him this evening?'

'No. The seat next to me was reserved for him but he didn't use it.'

'You weren't worried by that?'

'It wasn't my business to worry about Mr Migson.'

A silence. He had a way of clamping his fingertips to his temples and easing the skin up as if he wanted to make it baggier and more comfortable.

'Can you think of any reason why he should be wearing a replica of Lady Penwardine's stage costume?'

'No.'

That wasn't entirely true. I had the beginnings of a theory but no proof and I didn't want to start the police down that path until I'd reconnoitred it first.

'I gather from Lady Penwardine that the other costume

belonged to her as well.'

'Yes.'

'Did you ever see Mr Migson in or around Lady Penwardine's dressing room?'

'He walked past it yesterday. That's all, as far as I know.'

'Did any of the company express an opinion to you about Mr Migson?'

'I think we all regarded his presence here as ridiculous.'

'Did anybody in particular resent it?'

The answer to that was Charles and Bella, but I wasn't ready to give it.

'I don't think so.'

'What about Mr Shaw?'

'He seemed flattered, if anything. I don't think the Lord Chamberlain's ever sent his personal representative to take up residence with a production before.'

The inspector gave me another of his long looks when I said this. It rang an alarm bell.

'I suppose there's no doubt that he was from the Lord Chamberlain's department?'

'Why do you ask?'

'No particular reason, but we did all take him on trust when he arrived with his file full of corrections.'

'We're trying to find somebody from the Lord Chamberlain's office. It's not easy at this time of night.'

It was after eleven o'clock.

'I suppose you have no idea where Mr Migson lived or if he had any family?'

'No. I had very little to do with him. None of us did, as far as I know.'

There was a pause while the sergeant caught up with his notes.

I said: 'I suppose the shot I heard was the one that killed him. He couldn't have been in the basket all evening?'

I could see the inspector weighing up whether to respond or not. The scale came down slowly.

'One of the stage-hands looked inside the basket at about half-past seven. It was empty then. Also there's the blood.'

'Yes, I thought of that. If he'd been in there for long it would have started coagulating. There was no sign of that.'

Another sigh from him. The sergeant was looking at me oddly, but soon after that they let me go.

After trying a few doors unsuccessfully I found my way back to the dressing-room corridor to see if Bella needed help. When I knocked on her door it was Mercy Phipps who answered. I found her standing alone in what looked like a jumble sale.

'Where's Miss Flanagan?'

'She's gone, miss.'

Mercy's face was creased with worry. She had Bella's green suit in her arms. The ballooning costume was thrown over the chair. She saw my eyes going to it.

'Is it true he was wearing . . . her other one?'

'Yes.'

'Why, miss? Why would he do a thing like that?'

She seemed afraid she'd be blamed.

'I don't know.'

But whether I liked it or not the idea I hadn't mentioned to the inspector was taking shape in my mind. It involved Bella's belief that somebody at the theatre had been spying on her. If so, suppose there'd been a plan to sabotage the final scene of the play with a duplicate Cinderella wearing Bella's costume, guying Bella's movements, making the whole thing dissolve into farce.

'You say Miss Flanagan's gone. When?'

'About half an hour ago, miss. She came running in here, changed and sent me to ask the stage door-keeper to get her a cab.'

That must have been just after the inspector questioned her.

'Did she say where she was going?'

'No, miss.'

I assumed she'd gone home to Berkeley Square or possibly even to my house in Hampstead. I'd told her where I kept a spare key hidden for emergencies.

I'd left my hat in the green room. When I went back for it I found the population reduced to Charles, Vincent and the two Bonnets. Freeson was probably having his session with Inspector Merit.

Charles asked: 'Is Bella all right?'

'I've been looking for her. I think she must have gone home.'

I saw he wanted to ask more but couldn't because of the others. I collected my hat and went back along the dressing-room corridor, passing Mercy coming out of Bella's room with her green suit. She said she was taking it to her wardrobe room to press it. I was almost at the stage door when I heard a scream from behind me. Mercy's scream, shrill and terrified, going on and on.

I ran back along the corridor. A constable and a stage-hand came running from the other end, the constable blowing his whistle. All the time the screaming went on. A man in evening dress came backing out of the room it was coming from. He looked hunched, apologetic, but when he saw us he began to run, first towards me, then back towards the constable and the stage-hand. The three of us fell on him more or less together, knocking him over. He kicked and writhed but had no chance. The constable and the stage-hand dragged him to his feet. He hung limply between them, looking surprised at the noise and fuss.

'. . . in my wardrobe room. Hiding in my wardrobe room . . .' Mercy had stopped screaming and was trying to gasp out an explanation.

The man kept murmuring, 'I'm sorry. I'm sorry.'

His evening dress was looking much the worse for wear, tie undone, shirt front torn, jacket and overcoat hanging open. But then Piggy Ditchbrake could hardly be expected to look the picture of elegance after the kind of evening he'd spent. Inspector Merit arrived along with the sergeant, Freeson and the four actors from the green room.

Merit said: 'Who the devil is he?'

Piggy stared and said nothing. I had no reason to protect the man.

'His name's Piggy Ditchbrake. He's the friend of Lord Penwardine's I was telling you about.'

Piggy's stare transferred itself to me.

'What was he doing?' The inspector turned to Freeson. 'Has this man any business here?'

'Certainly not. He was one of the ringleaders of the trouble this evening. I thought he was thrown out.'

'He was,' I said. 'I helped throw him.'

'So what is he doing backstage now?'

Freeson said weakly, 'I suppose he must have come in again.'

He'd probably run straight round to the stage door while it was left unguarded. It linked with my idea that there'd been a scheme to sabotage the end of the play, involving Migson. I said nothing.

Inspector Merit glared at Piggy.

'Well, what are you doing here?'

Piggy said nothing either. He was panting and sweating heavily.

'You're under arrest. Keep him separate from the others. I'll speak to him when I've finished with Mr Freeson.'

Piggy found his voice, shrilly.

'Under arrest? Under arrest for being backstage in a theatre?'

'Under arrest for being found without explanation at the scene of a murder.'

'Murder?'

Piggy's eyes rolled. His mouth opened then clamped shut. He made no resistance as two police constables led him away.

'Now, Mr Freeson,' said the inspector, 'perhaps we can get on with our talk.'

As I left, the door-keeper was just letting in two men with a stretcher who'd come to take away Migson's body.

TEN

I WASN'T CONCERNED ABOUT Piggy Ditchbrake. He had as near an unbreakable alibi as anybody could need. Freeson had seen enough to explain that to the inspector and a night in the cells was the least he deserved. It was Bella I was worried about and I needed to find her. It was nearly midnight by now, with most of the theatre crowds gone home, no trams and few hansoms on the street. I decided to walk to Berkeley Square and set out at a good speed across Trafalgar Square and up Haymarket. The weather was turning colder and I noticed people huddled down for the night in doorways, wrapped in drifts of old clothes or the occasional tattered horse blanket.

As I walked I wondered if I might be lining up on the wrong side. I'd told Inspector Merit what I'd seen and heard but not in any way that would show him a pattern. But I thought a pattern was there. Lord Penwardine had been near the theatre before the play started. Piggy Ditchbrake had, for no obvious reason, come backstage immediately after being evicted from the front of the house. Matthew Migson – who might or might not be Lord Penwardine's spy – had been dressed in Bella's spare costume. All that pointed to a plan to sabotage the end of the play. And, in that case, who would have reason to shoot Migson?

Somebody who'd found out about the sabotage plan and resented it. And who would resent it most? One person above all and that person, if I didn't find her in Berkeley Square, was probably waiting at home for me in Hampstead. Whether she routinely carried a gun with her I didn't know, but it wouldn't surprise me. Was I obliged to be on Bella's side? Of course not. But it did seem to me that I had an obligation not to take sides against her until I knew more.

Going across Piccadilly Circus another unwelcome thought struck me. There'd been a gap of half an hour or so while we threw out the trouble-makers. And yet when I'd gone into Bella's dressing room towards the end of that time she was only just changing her costume. What had she been doing for thirty minutes with most of the lights out and confusion all round?

When I got to Berkeley Square I saw that the lights were on in most of Bella's windows but the ground-floor curtains were drawn. I walked up to the red front door, knocked and waited. After a long gap the butler opened it.

'I'd like to speak to Lady Penwardine. Would you please tell her that Nell Bray's here.'

'I'm sorry, madam, I regret Lady Penwardine is not at home.'

In butler language that only meant unwilling to see visitors.

'Will you at least send my name up please?'

'I'm sorry, madam, Lady Penwardine is not at home.' Then, with a slight change of voice, 'When I say not at home I mean her ladyship is not in residence.'

Then, over the butler's shoulder, I saw the plump maid Naomi coming downstairs with a leather dressing case in her hand. I thanked him and let him close the door on me.

If Bella had gone to my house she wouldn't need her dressing case. Her things were still there from the night before. Therefore Bella had gone, or was going, somewhere else. I walked down the steps and took a few turns round the square. Then I planted myself under a plane tree at the corner of the garden in the middle of the square so that I could keep an eye on Bella's front door. I wasn't exactly hiding, just being inconspicuous.

Twenty minutes passed. A clock struck half-past midnight. Frost was beginning to settle, sucking the damp out of the air, pinching the tips of my fingers even through leather gloves. A few hansoms went past. Then a lad who looked like a boot boy came up the steps from the basement of Bella's house and went running towards New Bond Street. When he came back a few minutes later there was a hansom cab ambling behind him. It stopped in front of the door. The maid Naomi came out in hat and coat, followed by the boot boy and another man carrying cases. Naomi and the luggage were loaded into the hansom and it set off in my direction.

There was no question of leaping into another hansom to follow them because the rest of the square was deserted. But it must have been a hard night for the cab horse because it ambled along as slowly as a circus elephant and the cab driver, with the class-consciousness of his kind, probably knew he only had a servant on board and made no attempt to hurry it. At a leisurely walk it turned into Mount Street towards Grosvenor Square. Equally leisurely, I followed on foot at about fifty yards' distance. It went across Grosvenor Square along Brook Street and into the comparative bustle of Park Lane. In spite of the lateness of the hour there was a stream of motor and horse-drawn vehicles on the road and I thought I'd lose it. But it went no more than a few hundred yards northwards before stopping in front of a narrow house with fancy white stonework over doors and windows, facing onto the park.

There was a lamp burning over the front door and plenty of lights on in the house, but the curtains were firmly drawn. It took Naomi and the cab driver two trips to get the cases up the steps. Then the cab ambled away and Naomi must have rung the bell because the door opened and she and the cases were hustled inside. From where I was standing I couldn't see who was on the inside of the door. I waited for a few minutes and then walked past the house. I could, I suppose, have tried walking up to the front door and asking for Lady Penwardine, but I didn't think it would do any good. Why on earth had Bella, in the middle of the night, decided to transfer herself across half a mile of London? The answer, I supposed, was that she had a dependable friend among the rich of Park Lane. That was all very well, but I wanted to know who it was.

I waited, collecting a suspicious look from a constable who probably thought I was a street-walker. I glared back at him. When he'd gone, a courting couple lingered, whispering and giggling, by the gatepost of the house next door. Eventually she kissed him and ran off down the basement steps. A servant girl going home late. I hoped a friend had left the scullery window open for her. The young man stood, staring after her. When I said good evening to him he jumped round, looking aggressive, but relaxed when he saw I had nothing to do with his girlfriend's household. I pointed to the house that interested me.

'I'm looking for a friend of mine. Can you tell me who lives there?'

He was surprised by my ignorance.

'That's Lord Penwardine's. You know, the one whose wife's gone off.'

He went away whistling, hands in pockets. I stayed, dumbfounded. Of all things I hadn't expected this, that Bella had fled back to her husband.

While I tried and failed to make sense of it another hansom arrived. This was a smarter affair, dashing along at a trot and pulling up so sharply that the horse reared its head up in protest. A man tumbled out, coat unbuttoned, top hat in hand. He pushed a fistful of money at the driver, who whipped up his horse and trotted off before he could be asked for change. Not that the new arrival was concerned with that. He came rushing across the pavement, then stopped short when he saw me.

'Nell Bray, what are you doing here?'

Charles Courts, looking and speaking like a man in a whirlwind.

'I should ask you the same.'

'Bella's in there.'

'So I gather. But how did you know?'

'I went to Berkeley Square as soon as the inspector finished with me. She wasn't there. Then I found out from the boot boy that she'd . . . she'd . . .'

He was gasping for breath. I don't suppose he ever dried up on stage, but he dried up then.

'That she'd gone back to her husband?'
'She wouldn't do that. She simply wouldn't do that.'
It came out as an angry shout.
'But it seems she has. This is Lord Penwardine's house.
I've just watched Bella's maid go into it with her luggage.
What other interpretation is there?'
'He's kidnapped her.'
I tried to make allowances for actor's temperament.
'I shouldn't have thought a woman who'd been
kidnapped would send for her maid and a cab full of
luggage.'
'He must have forced her to do it.'
'Bella doesn't strike me as a woman who'd be easily
forced to do anything.'
'He's a ruthless man.'
His hair was flopping round his face, his eyes wild. A
matinee audience would have loved it.
'I'm going to insist on seeing her.'
'How?'
'I'm simply going to walk up and bang on the front
door.'
He did. Reasoning with him would have been like trying
to persuade Romeo not to climb the balcony. Or Macbeth
to ignore Lady Macbeth. I wished that second idea hadn't
come to me, but there was no doing away with it.
The door stayed closed against him. He knocked again,
then again. A curtain twitched in a downstairs window.
The fourth knock was long and thunderous. After a while
the door was opened by a nervous-looking butler. Charles
said something short that I couldn't hear from the
pavement. The butler's reply was shorter. The door
slammed. Charles resumed pounding on the knocker as if
he intended to force it straight through the door. The
blinds went up in the house next door but there was no
further movement of the curtains in Lord Penwardine's
house.
Charles was shouting at the closed door: 'I will not go
away. I will not go away.'
I saw, though he couldn't, two burly men walking up the
basement steps to the side of the front door. They looked

like outdoor servants and they were fidgeting with their arms and shoulders the way men do before action.

'Charles,' I shouted. 'Come away, for goodness sake.'

He didn't hear me. The two men crept up the steps behind him, grabbed him by the shoulders and threw him down. Before I could get to him he was on his feet and up the steps again. The two men were waiting for him. He hit one of them on the chin, throwing him with a thump against the door. The second man took a mighty swipe at him and connected with the side of the head just above the ear. Charles staggered and the second man caught him and threw him down the steps again.

This time I got to him just as he was trying to get up. He looked dazed but still furious.

'Will you please let go of me? I'm not . . .'

Heavy steps on the gravel.

'What's all this then?'

The same policeman who'd taken me for a street-walker. Goodness knows what he thought now. I did my best for Charles.

'This gentleman has been manhandled. He needs medical help. If you could find a cab for us . . .'

It might have worked except Charles decided to take a speaking part.

'There's a lady in that house who's been kidnapped. They won't let me see her.'

The constable's face changed and I really couldn't blame him. Lying on the ground in Park Lane and shouting at one o'clock in the morning, with your shirt front torn and your clothes all over the place, is no way to convince a policeman that you're sober.

'That will be quite enough of that, sir. Is this gentleman a friend of yours, miss?'

'Yes. I'll see he . . .'

The front door of Lord Penwardine's house opened just long enough to let out the unhappy-looking butler. He came towards us but stopped at a safe distance from Charles, who was now on his feet.

He said to the constable: 'It's about time one of you got here.'

'Has this gentleman been causing a nuisance?'

'He certainly has. He's been standing on the step trying to knock a hole through the front door and uttering threats.'

I said: 'It was nowhere near as bad as that. He was simply . . .'

'I demand to speak to Lady Penwardine.'

This last contribution was a shout from Charles to the butler and it destroyed any hope he might have had of avoiding a night in the cells. The constable gave him a shocked look, as if shouting a lady's name in Park Lane was definitely one of the things not done, and clipped a handcuff on his wrist. Charles looked from the handcuff to the constable to me as if bewildered by this turn of events. I had one last try.

'I'm sure there's no need for that, officer. If you'll just let him go away quietly . . .'

'I will not go away quietly. I will not go anywhere until . . .'

For the second time that night a policeman's whistle shrilled in my ears. Another two police constables came running. Charles, still protesting, was dragged away. One of the burly men who'd watched with interest from the bottom of the steps melted back into the basement. The butler practically ran back up the steps and the front door opened a crack to let him in and closed quickly. The front of Lord Penwardine's town house was as uncommunicative as the face of a cliff.

ELEVEN

I TOOK A CAB HOME and managed a few hours sleep in my own bed. In the morning curiosity drove me back to the Crispin Theatre. The stage door-keeper lowered his racing paper as I came in.

'I hear they've let him go.'

'Who?'

'That toff they found in here last night.'

'Who told you?'

'One of the constables. The inspector's been looking for you.'

I hoped it had no connection with Charles' performance in Park Lane. I went to the room behind the box office and knocked on the door. Inspector Merit's voice told me to come in. He was on his own, sitting at the desk with no sign of work or notes in front of him. He looked weary and was still wearing the same shirt as the night before.

'I gather you wanted to see me.'

He gave me a long unblinking look, not hostile but not friendly either. I sat down.

'You were wrong about seeing Lord Penwardine, you know. He spent all of yesterday evening at home.'

'Did he tell you that?'

Another look, a shade reproachful this time. I don't know if it implied that a peer of the realm would never tell a lie or that it wouldn't be easy for the police to prove it if he did.

'His mother vouches for it. Also several of the domestic staff.'

'Of course.'

'In any case, Lord Penwardine crossing the Strand

wouldn't have helped us with a shooting in the theatre a good hour and a half later, would it?'

'So you think that sound we took for a firecracker was the shot that killed Migson?'

He was doing his skin-stretching act again, creasing his forehead with his fingers.

'There's no evidence to the contrary. Mr Migson was shot in the back by a bullet from a pistol. It penetrated his heart. The first constable on the scene reports that the body was still warm. How long would that be from the time you think your heard the shot?'

I thought back. When the curtain rose again there was about half an hour of the play to go.

'No more than fifty minutes, I'd say. The producer, Mr Freeson, might have a more accurate idea.'

'We've talked to him again this morning. He agrees with you.'

He sat there, elbows on desk, chin in hands, staring at me with his froglike eyes. It was as if he expected me, out of pure pity, to give him a fact like a plump fly to gulp down. I didn't oblige.

'Was he shot inside the balloon basket?'

'There are traces of blood on the rim of it and on one side. But those might have been made when the actors lifted him out. It's a pity they moved him.'

'But it's possible that somebody shot him first and then put him in there?'

'They say all things are possible.'

Then, after a long silence:

'Miss Bray, you were here when Mr Migson first arrived at the dress rehearsal. Would you please tell me what you can remember about it?'

This was interesting. It suggested that he too thought there might be something odd about Migson's presence. I gave him a summary of most of the things I could remember.

'And Mr Migson clearly stated that he had been told by the Lord Chamberlain to remain with the production?'

'As far as I remember, Mr Shaw was the one who announced it, but Mr Migson was standing beside him at the time and he agreed it was right.'

'And the actors were surprised by that?'

'We were all surprised. As Mr Shaw pointed out, it had never happened before.'

'I see.'

I said: 'Do I take it that Matthew Migson wasn't from the Lord Chamberlain's office after all?'

'Oh, he was certainly from the Lord Chamberlain's office. He was one of the clerks to the Examiner of Plays.'

'But . . .?'

'But he'd simply been told to deliver the Lord Chamberlain's corrections to the theatre, then go back to his office. There'd never been any intention that he should stay.'

He watched my face.

'That doesn't seem to surprise you.'

'Didn't his office miss him?'

'Until we were in touch with them early this morning, they assumed he'd been taken ill. You haven't answered my question.'

'Was it a question? No, it doesn't surprise me very much. There seemed something odd about Mr Migson.'

'The question is, what was the man doing here? Nobody seems able to tell me that.'

His voice was plaintive. I had to resist the temptation to feed him. If I told him my suspicion that Migson had been employed by Lord Penwardine to spy on Bella and Charles and sabotage the production it might promote the pair of them up the list of suspects. I wanted to know more before I did that. Also, I was annoyed with him for not believing me about Lord Penwardine.

'Did you try asking Piggy Ditchbrake?'

'Why?'

'Don't you think it's an interesting coincidence that both he and Mr Migson were backstage, where they had no business to be?'

'Mr Ditchbrake assured us that he'd never met Mr Migson.'

'Did he tell you what he was doing backstage?'

He sighed. I guessed he was being patient with me in the

hope of being fed his fly, but was finding it a strain.

'Strictly speaking Miss Bray, I should tell you that it's no business of yours. I gather that Mr Ditchbrake resented being ejected and took the first opportunity of getting in again.'

'So you let him go?'

'We had very little choice in the matter. I understand you actually had a hand on his arm when you heard the shot from behind the curtain.'

'Yes.'

'It's up to the theatre, of course, to consider whether they want to bring an action against Mr Ditchbrake for trespass.'

'And of course he has powerful friends.'

'Has he?'

He gave me another of his unblinking looks, seeming prepared to sit there all day if necessary. He was inactive for a man in charge of a murder inquiry, as if all the information he needed would eventually come floating to him of its own accord. That worried me. I asked if he had anything else he wanted to ask me.

'Not for the moment, Miss Bray. Not for the moment.'

On the way out the door-keeper put down his mug of tea and asked if they'd arrested anybody yet.

I still wanted to speak to Bella but didn't fancy my chances of storming the Penwardine house. On the other hand my experience of London police courts told me exactly where I was likely to find Charles. I took a tram to Great Marlborough Street and had no trouble finding a place in the public gallery. There was a fat woman with a heavy cold on one side of me, an old man sucking cough sweets on the other. On the bench a weary stipendiary magistrate dealt with the glum procession of overnight cases. It took on average about three minutes to bring the next prisoner up from the cells, dispense what passed for justice and send him or her down again. Drunk and disorderly, fined forty shillings or five days. Repeated soliciting, fourteen days without the option. The accused looked pinched with cold and hopelessness, the court ushers and the police not much better.

Charles Courts' case came immediately after the one for selling clockwork parrots without a street-trading licence. The tattered hawker went down from the dock and up came an almost equally tattered Charles. He was unshaven, his jacket minus several buttons, and his shirt was held together by a safety pin. When the clerk of the court asked his name he gave it with the air of Sidney Carton at the guillotine, only gloomier. It was lucky for him that this routine sitting had attracted no newspaper reporters. He frowned when he saw me.

I mouthed at him: 'Plead guilty.'

The court usher gave me a sharp look, but it was enough. As an actor he'd learned to take his cue. The charge was put to him and he admitted his guilt with a questioning glance at me. The police constable rattled through an approximation of the event. The magistrate said, in a voice so weary it could scarcely struggle out of his mouth:

'Forty shillings or five days.'

Charles, with a dazed look on his face, like Hamlet who's just been told that soliloquies are out of fashion, was taken down from the dock to pay his fine.

I was waiting by the side door when he came out ten minutes later, bare-headed, overcoat collar turned up and disposed to be argumentative.

'I was not drunk. Why did you tell me to plead guilty?'

'Because if you'd said not guilty you'd have had to explain your side of what happened. If you'd tried to tell the magistrate you thought Lady Penwardine had been kidnapped by her husband you'd have ended up in prison and all over the papers.'

'But if she'd gone with him of her own free will, why wouldn't they let me speak to her? I'm going back there now.'

'At least have some coffee first.'

After the sort of coffee they provide in police cells I knew that would be irresistible. He let me propel him towards a corner café. His hands were bare and pink in the cold.

'I've lost my gloves, my hat. There were thieves in there, drunks. It was like something out of Dante.'

He drank two cups of coffee and ate most of a Chelsea

bun. I found myself liking the man much more in his subdued state. By cold morning light in the wreckage of evening dress, with some of the gloss of confidence taken off him, his looks were a pleasure rather than an annoyance. Warning bell. There should be at least one woman in London who was not in love with Charles Courts and I hoped I knew my duty.

I told him I'd been to the theatre.

'Was she there?'

'No.'

'Did anybody know anything about her?'

'I didn't have much chance to ask. Inspector Merit wanted to see me again.'

'I don't like that man. What did he want?'

'He wanted to find out what Migson was doing at the Crispin.'

'Well, he knew that, didn't he?'

'We all thought we knew, but apparently we were wrong. Migson was only supposed to deliver the script changes. The Lord Chamberlain hadn't told him to attach himself to us.'

'Then what was he doing?'

'I wondered if you might perhaps have some ideas about that.'

There was quite a long hesitation then, rather weakly: 'What do you mean?'

'Do you know what Migson was really doing?'

'What is this? Are you working for the police?'

He was trying to be angry, but I sensed fear.

'I'm not working for anybody, but I object to being cast as a walk-on player in other people's dramas. You were angry when Migson arrived, weren't you?'

'We were all angry. It was an insult to us as artists.'

When people take a high tone, I know they're struggling. His face was full of annoyance and bewilderment, rather over-acted, but then he wasn't used to making his effects across a café table.

'I think you had a suspicion from the start that Migson wasn't quite what he claimed to be. I think you guessed what he was doing there.'

He could hold a silence, another actor's gift. He kept it for a count of ten or more. Then:

'Really? What was that?'

'You thought he'd been sent to spy on you and Bella Flanagan.'

His body jerked with surprise. Almost at once he brought it under control and sipped at the dregs of his coffee.

'Two questions arise from that,' I said. 'The first is, were you right?'

'And the second?'

'Did you kill him?'

He looked at me, then, slowly, began to smile. It looked like a real smile as if, in spite of everything, something had happened to please him.

'No, I didn't.'

'Where were you in that long interval?'

'I stayed in my dressing room. There didn't seem to be any point in going out and adding to the confusion.'

I said quietly, so that people at the other tables didn't hear: 'Mr Courts, you're a liar and not a very good one.'

'Why do you say that?'

'Look at the circumstances. There's a near riot going on. You've just had some of the worst few minutes you've ever experienced on stage . . .'

'Oh, I shouldn't say that. At Cambridge once we . . .'

'Don't change the subject. You'd had, at any rate, a bad few minutes by any standards. And if it was bad for you it must have been very much worse for Bella, who hadn't been on stage before.'

'I grant you that.'

'And you, to say the least, are concerned about Bella. So what do you do?'

'Well?'

'One thing you don't do is sit there in your dressing room with Bella only a few doors away down the corridor and not look in to try and reassure her. It would be a civility to any leading lady. Surely you'd do as much for Bella?'

He was shaken now and couldn't hide it.

84

'I think you did go to her dressing room at least once, didn't you?'

'Yes, I suppose I did.'

'Suppose you did?'

'Yes.'

'And what happened?'

'She wasn't there.'

He leaned back in his chair as if all the tiredness from the night before had come over him in a wave.

'Was anybody else there?'

'The wardrobe mistress, Mercy.'

'Did she know where Bella was?'

He shook his head.

'Was that why you were so anxious to speak to Bella last night?'

He burst out: 'She had nothing to do with it. Nothing to do with it at all.'

'But you wanted to hear that from Bella in person?'

'I wanted to know what she was doing. She'd never go back to that man of her own free will. Never.'

The café was filling up. Eyes were beginning to turn in our direction. He stood up, rattling cups on the table.

'I'm going back there, Miss Bray. I'm going to speak to Bella if I have to pull down every stone in Park Lane to get to her.'

TWELVE

IT WAS A GOOD EXIT line and he went. I settled the bill and caught up with him a few hundred yards down the street.

'If you're arrested again it will be fourteen days without the option.'

That slowed him down.

'Well, what do you suggest?'

I wanted to speak to Bella too. We were allies to that extent at least.

'Houses have back entrances. We might find out more there.'

'I refuse to hang around back doors gossiping to servants.'

'Even if the alternative is being thrown down the front steps by them?'

He saw the point. We took a hansom to Park Lane. I had to pay because he'd spent most of his ready money on the fine. It was becoming an expensive operation.

We got out some distance from Lord Penwardine's house. As we walked towards it I noticed a small turning littered with straw and horse droppings.

'A mews. That's what we want.'

I nudged Charles towards it. He was still showing a tendency to march up to the front door and there was a policeman on the other side of the road. It was the conventional mews cul-de-sac that you find behind most big London houses, with a line of two-storey brick buildings looking and smelling surprisingly rustic in the fashionable heart of town. Hay and straw bales bulged from openings in the upper storeys. A pair of bay heads looked out of adjoining boxes. A groom was sluicing down the cobbles with buckets of water.

'Is this Lord Penwardine's stables?'

'Urrgh.'

Either he had no roof to his mouth or he always growled at strangers. Either way, not promising. We had to jump back when he threw the next bucketful.

The next building in the row had changed from stables to garage. A chauffeur in jodhpurs and hacking jacket, as if he still had horses to deal with, was lovingly polishing the headlamps of a glossy red car. Charles brightened up at once.

'Now that looks better.'

'It might not be Lord Penwardine's.'

'It's not. Bella told me he sticks to horses. But have you noticed, grooms hardly ever talk and chauffeurs never stop?'

He walked confidently up to the car and presumably made some intelligent mechanical remark, because the chauffeur straightened up, all smiles. When I followed, he and Charles were talking gear ratios like long-lost brothers.

'Have you tried her on any long journeys?'

'A bit longer than yours anyway, sir. What was it, twenty-nine miles before you crashed?'

Charles laughed. Being in contact with a machine seemed to have cheered him up no end.

'I wouldn't call it a crash, more of an emergency landing.'

'Rather you than me, anyway, sir. I thought I recognised you from the picture in the *Daily Mail*. The future is in the skies, you said.'

'Well, it is. Another ten years and the motor car will be obsolete. If you want to go from London to Edinburgh for lunch you'll just get into your aeroplane and fly there.'

This was all very well, but hardly inconspicuous. I'd forgotten that to some crazy enthusiasts Charles was better known as a pioneer aviator than an actor.

I said: 'Is that Lord Penwardine's stables next door?'

'That's it, ma'am, and a bloody nuisance they are. One of his nags tried to kick our radiator when they came back this morning.'

'They've been out this morning already then?'

'Three times. Mud and straw all over the place. Mucky things, horses.'

This, loud enough to be heard by the man sluicing the cobbles, was clearly part of a continuing battle. Charles, distracted from the car, took up the questioning.

'Three times? Where did they go?'

His tone was sharp. Luckily the chauffeur was too admiring to notice.

'Paddington. That's where they go from when they're moving down to his estate in Berkshire. The staff went off at the crack of dawn with the luggage, then his lordship and the two ladies just after breakfast.'

'Two ladies?'

This time even the chauffeur noticed. I gave Charles a warning glance.

'Lord Penwardine, his mother Lady Dorothea and the young Lady Penwardine. You know, the American one there was all the fuss over. She was supposed to have gone away, but anyway she's back now.'

I said hastily, to stop Charles making a fool of himself: 'How did she look?'

He thought about it.

'Well, you wouldn't say she was one of the world's great beauties, not with hair that colour, but there's something about her. She always used to pass the time of day with me when she was living here. Not the other two, though. He's as proud as the Emperor of Russia and his mother's worse.'

'Did Lady Penwardine say anything to you this morning?'

Charles was leaning forward, trying to nudge me aside.

'Oh yes, we had quite a long talk while he was getting Lady Dorothea settled in the carriage. She had a bad back and the groom had to go and look for a clean rug to make a pad for it. So Lady Penwardine came over for a look at the car.'

'What did she talk about?'

'She commented on the weather being colder. She asked if motor cars are harder to start in cold weather. She said she'd been thinking of buying one.'

88

'Yes, she had.'

This from Charles, a kind of groan in my ear.

'Then what happened?'

'They got the old lady settled, he helped Lady Penwardine into the carriage and off they went.'

Charles asked: 'She didn't seem reluctant to go?'

I could feel the effort it cost him to keep his voice calm.

'No, I wouldn't say so. She just said goodbye to me and went.'

I could feel Charles' tensed muscles slump.

I said: 'What about the third time?'

'Oh, that was the eloping couple.'

'Eloping?'

He laughed.

'Not really. That was just what I called them in my own mind. It did seem a bit odd, though. This gentleman came skulking along here, still in evening dress at ten o'clock in the morning but no hat or scarf, just the overcoat. He cadges a cigarette off Happy Harry the groom there, then Harry opens the carriage door for him and drives him off, cool as if he owned it.'

'Was he plump, quite young, brown hair and a very red face?'

'That's the one. You know him, ma'am?'

'I've met him a couple of times. And the woman?'

'She was waiting for him on the corner there. He opened the door and she nipped in beside him.'

'What did she look like?'

'I only saw the back of her. Not as tall as you are. Fur hat.'

I said we must go, although Charles seemed reluctant to drag himself away from the place where Bella had been. The chauffeur deferentially asked him for his autograph and Charles obliged like a man in a dream. I guided him back towards Park Lane.

As soon as we were out of the chauffeur's hearing he said, sounding angry at me:

'What was all that about? Who were these other people?'

'I don't know who the woman was. The man was certainly Piggy Ditchbrake after the police let him go. If he can commandeer Lord Penwardine's carriage like that, there must be a close connection.'

That didn't seem to interest him.

I said: 'At least that cleared up one thing. Bella went off with her husband of her own free will.'

'I don't believe it. She simply would not do it.'

Troilus deserted by Cressida couldn't have been more incredulous.

'Look, she was talking to that chauffeur long enough to discuss how you start a car in cold weather. He obviously likes her and doesn't like Lord Penwardine. Wouldn't that be her perfect opportunity to get a message to somebody if she were being held against her will?'

We walked towards Marble Arch. Charles was attracting glances from the combination of his looks and his bedraggled clothes.

I said: 'So they're going to his country estate. Whereabouts in Berkshire?'

'It's called Ockton Hall, in the Vale of the White Horse. Not far from where . . .'

He stopped suddenly.

'Where what?'

'Oh nothing.'

At Marble Arch we parted after, with some embarrassment, he'd borrowed five shillings off me for a cab fare. I had a meeting of the Women's Social and Political Union in Clement's Inn that I couldn't miss, murder or no murder. I waited at the tram stop and watched him striding away down Oxford Street. Heads turned after him as he went, but he didn't seem to notice.

THIRTEEN

IT WAS AN INTENSE MEETING, quite grim enough to put
out of my head for a while the affairs of the Crispin
Theatre. We had two delegates from Newcastle with us,
reporting on the treatment of hunger strikers in prison
there. Then we started discussing the next demonstration
outside Parliament and got embroiled in the minor
disagreements about tactics that always cause more trouble
than the big issues. By lunchtime, when we took a break
for cups of rather watery coffee, we'd more or less argued
ourselves to a halt and conversation became more relaxed.
Except as far as I was concerned.

Two of my colleagues on the committee had been at the
Crispin the night before and wanted to know more. One
of them produced a copy of the *Daily Mail*, explaining
hastily that it wasn't her usual paper but she'd seen
something on the placard about theatre death. The
paragraph on page two came as something of a relief. It
said simply that a man had been killed in an accident
backstage during a disturbance at the first night of a new
play by George Bernard Shaw. The leading part in the
play was performed by Lady Penwardine. The identity of
the victim had not been disclosed.

It was evidently all Fleet Street had been able to find out
from the police at midnight, but it would be more than
enough to start the rest of the press pack on the trail. My
friends, though, weren't concerned about the identity of
the victim. What they wanted to know was whether Shaw
had suddenly deserted the cause.

'That ending, Nell. Surely he didn't write it like that?'

'No, it's all right. She doesn't really go running back to

91

her husband. Only . . .'

I stopped. This was likely to be complicated, but the word would get out in any case.

'Only what?'

'Well, I'm afraid in real life that's exactly what she seems to have done.'

They were more shocked at the idea that Bella had gone back to an unsatisfactory husband than they would have been if I'd told them about the murder. A few of them, it turned out, had spoken to Bella at meetings and regarded her as politically naive but essentially sound. Also, her status as victim of our unfair divorce laws gave her celebrity of a kind.

'After all, it's an open secret that Penwardine's been unfaithful to her practically from the time they walked out of Westminster Abbey together. I've heard he keeps the other woman in a cottage on his estate.'

'Yes, and there's nothing she can do about it. Whereas he can throw her aside for looking at another man.'

'Well, it would take a bit more than looking.'

A disapproving cough from Emmeline told us we'd passed the boundary between social concern and common gossip.

'Whatever has to be done, I'm sure Nell will deal with it. Now, are we agreed on the wording of the message we're sending back to Newcastle?'

It seemed I'd been given orders of a kind, and that they amounted to looking after Bella. It was certainly not the time and place to mention my worries about what she'd been doing the night before.

Later in the afternoon, when the meeting was over, I went back to the Crispin Theatre. A man was pasting diagonal strips reading 'Further Performances Postponed' across the posters for *Cinderella Revisited*. A group of journalists, some with cameras, were waiting outside the stage door. Several knew me from rallies and demonstrations.

'Miss Bray, is it true Lady Penwardine has gone back to her husband?'

'Nell, have the police questioned you yet?'

'Is it true Bernard Shaw's shot the Lord Chamberlain?'

I advised them to ask Inspector Merit. The door-keeper, grown conscientious at last, opened the door a crack to let me in. I asked what was happening.

'Nothing much, except the bloody journalists. There was a bit of excitement this morning when they found his clothes, but the inspector's gone away again now.'

'Whose clothes?'

'Him who got murdered. Migson's.'

'Where were they?'

'In the chorus dressing room, the one at the far end. The police are in there now with Mr Freeson.'

I took that for an invitation and went along the corridor, my footsteps sounding hollow in the emptiness. There was a desolate feeling in the theatre that came not from the abrupt ending to a life but the equally abrupt ending to the run of a play. A door at the far end was open with lights and voices coming from it. I paused in the doorway. It was a big, bare room with mirrors, a rough wooden counter and a few electric lights down one side of it, a line of clothes stands down the other. When the Crispin was staging musical comedies it would be full of the noise and smells of the chorus changing in a hurry. Now there was only Freeson and a police sergeant holding up a black overcoat.

'And this was the one he was wearing when he came in, sir?'

'Yes, it looks like it. I've already told the inspector.'

Freeson sounded even wearier than usual.

'I'm sorry, sir, but we have to go through it all properly for the evidence.'

Freeson saw me and said good afternoon. He seemed to take it for granted that I should be there and even looked relieved.

The sergeant folded up the overcoat and draped it over the edge of an open tea chest standing on the floor. On the bare counter, under the electric lights, were a black jacket, pinstriped trousers, a watch and watch chain, a shirt. The sergeant made no protest when I walked over to them. Picking up the shirt, a plain one in white cotton, a feeling of Migson's humanity hit me, which was more than it had done while the man was alive.

'He certainly took this off in a hurry.'

The sleeves were pulled inside out, the celluloid cuffs that clerks wear to protect their shirts from ink-stains still clinging to them. Usually a man careful enough to wear celluloid cuffs will remove them before he takes off his shirt.

Freeson said: 'They were all on the floor, all his clothes, just as he must have left them.'

He sounded scared and rather sad, as if Migson's reality had struck him as well.

'So he must have rushed in here, presumably carrying Bella's spare costume, changed into it in a hurry and left his clothes anyhow. What about boots?'

The sergeant said, deadpan: 'He was wearing those. And his socks.'

That made sense. He might have been small enough to fit into Bella's costume, but not her silver boots. Trousers, jacket and waistcoat went into the tea chest. The sergeant paused with the watch and chain in his hand.

'Nice watch. He must have been in a hurry to leave that lying around.'

'Is there any inscription?'

He turned it over and opened it.

'No. A few pawnbroker's marks, that's all.'

So Migson had been hard up. Hard up enough to accept Lord Penwardine's bribe?

The sergeant stood there with the watch, looking round the bare room for something to wrap it in. Finding nothing, he burrowed in the pocket of Migson's overcoat and came out with a handkerchief, creased and ink-stained. Suitably wrapped, the watch went into the chest.

'I suppose all this will be going to his next-of-kin eventually. Was he married?'

The sergeant shook his head.

'Not as far as we know. He lived in lodgings in Holborn.'

He ticked off items on a list, picked up the tea chest and carried it along the corridor to the stage door. Its

94

immediate destination, I supposed, was some room half a mile away in Scotland Yard. Evidence of what we knew already, that at some point on the last evening of his life Migson had changed out of his clerk's clothes and into the Cinderella flying costume he was wearing when he died. Why?

Freeson bent to pick up something from the floor, a scrap of paper the colour of corned beef.

'What's that?'

'A theatre ticket, by the look of it. It must have fallen out of Migson's pocket when the sergeant pulled out the handkerchief.'

'One of yours?'

'No.'

He gave it to me. It said, in coarse black type, 'Marquesa's'. Then the previous Thursday's date. Nothing else.

'I've never heard of Marquesa's. Is it a theatre?'

'No. A music hall perhaps, or something amateur.'

I slipped it into my pocket, intending to give it to the sergeant on the way out.

Freeson switched off the lights and closed the door behind us. He hesitated in the corridor and I sensed that he was at a loss now that the play had suddenly been taken away from him. He invited me into his office for a cup of tea. He had a small fire there and a kettle on it close to boiling. When the tea was brewing he fidgeted around for a while, then came out with what was worrying him.

'I do hope Mr Shaw doesn't think it was my fault.'

'Of course he doesn't. How could he?'

'It was my first production with him, you see. I've always wanted to work with him, and now all this.'

I consoled him as best I could and brought the conversation round to what interested me.

'Had you ever met Matthew Migson before?'

He shook his head. Then he burst out suddenly:

'What was he doing here? What on earth did he think he was doing?'

He was angry with Migson for getting himself murdered and spoiling his production.

I said: 'Whatever he was doing, we know it wasn't on behalf of the Lord Chamberlain.'

He nodded. The inspector had told him about that.

'If we knew more about him we might know what he was doing.'

He took the bait.

'How could we find out?'

'Do you happen to know anybody else from the Lord Chamberlain's office?'

He thought for a moment.

'There was a man I met once. I didn't like him much, though.'

'Never mind if you liked him, would he talk to us?'

'He'd talk to anybody who'd buy him a drink.'

Which was how, at ten-past six, I found myself sitting in the saloon bar of a public house with Freeson and the man who'd known Matthew Migson. He wasn't, at first or even second glance, the kind of man you'd expect to work for the official examiner of plays. He was a plump, broad-shouldered young man of about the same age as Migson, but physically as unlike him as could be. Although he wore the same clerk's uniform of black jacket and striped trousers that I'd seen folded into the tea chest, he managed to give them a raffish air, like a silver ring bookmaker. He'd shown some surprise when Freeson and I met him as he came out of the Lord Chamberlain's office but the invitation to a drink had been instantly accepted. The first half of his pint disappeared at a gulp while Freeson sipped at a glass of stout and I drank sherry. Freeson had introduced the other man simply as Ted and informed him that I was a friend of Mr Shaw's.

Ted gave a sigh of satisfaction as the beer hit his stomach, wiped the back of his hand across his mouth and said:

'So who shot poor little Migson?'

Freeson left it to me to reply. Nobody knew, I said.

'I'm making a book on it. I'm offering five-to-one on George Bernard Shaw.'

'Do I gather Matthew Migson wasn't a close friend of yours?'

'I don't think he was a close friend of anybody's.'

He drank more beer.

'Did he have a family?'

'None that he ever talked about. I know both his parents were dead.'

'And no close friends?'

'No. Kept himself to himself, did little Migson. He wasn't what you'd call popular in the office. Took the job too seriously for one thing.'

'You don't?'

'Ye gods, no. How could you? Sitting there day after day combing through piles of boring play scripts in case somebody puts his hand on a girl's titties, or even mentions them. You'd think . . . Sorry, forgot I was talking to a lady. Another drink?'

He half stood up, but took care to let Freeson win the race to the bar.

'Go on forgetting it.'

'I mean, it's not a job you'd choose if you could help it, is it? I'm only here because I got flung out of Oxford in my second year when the proctors found I was keeping a race horse.'

He drained his glass and instantly transferred his hand to the full one Freeson had just put on the table.

'To be honest, it was a syndicate. I only owned the two front legs. Damned slow legs at that.'

'Were the hind legs any faster?'

He gulped with laughter, sending beer spray flying.

'You were saying Migson took the job seriously?'

'Oh yes. He'd sit there with his glasses gleaming and his nose twitching and whenever he found anything that might just offend a ninety-year-old narrow-minded nun, he'd be bouncing around in his seat like the school sneak. "Please sir, I've found something nasty, sir." Couldn't stand him, to be honest.'

'I gather he was off work without permission all yesterday and the afternoon before.'

'Yes, that was unusual. Always present, always punctual, little pink fingernails clean as a whistle, that was our Migson.'

'Did he have any money problems?'

'Not that I know of. He was as tight as the back end of a ... I mean, he wasn't what you'd call generous with his money.'

'Women friends?'

'Never mentioned any. Besides, what girl would go out with the likes of little Migson?'

He pulled out his pocket watch and downed the remains of his second pint.

'Got to go. Got to see a man about a gee gee.'

I said on an impulse: 'Did he ever talk about somewhere called Marquesa's?'

I'd been fingering the ticket in my pocket. I hadn't had a chance to give it to the sergeant.

Ted was already on his feet, putting an arm into his overcoat sleeve. He wrinkled his forehead.

'Marquesa's? No, I don't think I ever heard him mention it.'

'But you've heard the name?'

'It rings a faint bell. I've an idea it might be one of the old pub music halls in the East End, out the Mile End Road way.'

'The sort of place you'd expect Migson to go to?'

'Wouldn't have thought so.'

He told Freeson he'd see him again soon and hurried out, the door swinging behind him and letting in blasts of cold evening air. I looked at Freeson, still sipping his first stout.

'Do you fancy a trip to the music hall?' I said.

FOURTEEN

I DIDN'T NEED A GUIDE to the East End of London after all our political campaigning there. Still, a man was a useful accessory when wandering round it after dark. We took one of the new electric trams to the Mile End Road and the smooth gliding, in contast to the jolts of the horse trams, made the transition from west to east seem easy but odd, like a dream. There's a line as you travel east where the electric lights in shop windows and outside public houses give place to gas, a shift from white to a soft yellow that seems to bring its own mist with it, whatever the weather is doing elsewhere.

People behave differently too. As the colour of the light changes you see more of them on the streets. The November cold that drives West Enders inside their clubs and houses seems to have less effect on East Enders. They hang about on street corners or in the light of pub doorways, not doing anything very much, just looking. In more prosperous districts children are tidied away at the onset of dark, but here they were still loose around the streets, running errands, waiting around pie shops looking hopeful.

Freeson stared out of the tram window as if all this were new to him. I was glad he hadn't asked why we were doing this because I wasn't sure myself. But if Migson had been a spy or saboteur in the pay of Lord Penwardine there must have been some connecting line between them. The idea of the remote and aristocratic Penwardine doing his own bribery and corruption was out of the question. As Bella said, the servants did the dirty work. But if a friend like, for instance, Piggy Ditchbrake had been sent to give instructions to Migson, an obscure music hall might be as good a place as any. I hoped, none too confidently, that I might find somebody who'd recognise a description of Migson or Piggy.

When we got off in Whitechapel at the western end of Mile End Road, Freeson stood like a man in hostile territory.

'What do we do now?'

I went up to a group of men round a jellied-eel stand and asked if they knew of the Marquesa music hall. Most of them looked blank, but one of the younger ones said it might be the hall at the back of the Black Swan, first right, then second left. I thought he gave me an odd look when he said it. While I was there I bought two portions of jellied eels and mashed potatoes, and handed one of them to Freeson. He shied like a pony.

'What are we going to do with those?'

'You can do what you like with yours. I'm going to eat mine.'

We stood there under a street lamp and ate them. The eels were good and meaty, with a hint of parsley in the rich jelly, the potatoes hot and silky smooth. I took the plates back to the stall and we went on our way.

The Black Swan turned out to be a pub much like others in the area, with an ornate frontage in moulded brick including a black-painted swan marooned in its pool of lamplight twenty feet above the pavement. There was no sign of a music hall but, as we watched, two women in frothing feathered hats and velvet cloaks, with a small man walking between them like a prisoner, turned into an alleyway at the side. We lost sight of them, but a burst of music flared out and was cut off suddenly, suggesting a door had been opened for them.

'Come on,' I said.

Freeson fell reluctantly into step beside me down the alleyway.

'I thought all these sort of places had been closed down years ago.'

The music hall was a rectangular building with small windows set high in the walls that reminded me of a

Sunday school. I pushed open the door and felt the weight of bodies pressing against it from the inside, glimpsed bright gas lamps and velvet and ostrich feathers. On the platform at the far end a man in evening dress was singing. Then our way was blocked by a large muscular man in tweed jacket and cap.

'How many of you?'

'Two.'

'Two quid.'

That would have been expensive at the plushest music hall in the West End, let alone here. Still, there was no point in arguing and I couldn't expect Freeson to pay. As I passed over the money I thought the man was looking at Freeson and me as if making sure he'd know us again. In spite of the music and warmth wafting to us from inside, there was an edgy feel about the place. The question of what a prim little clerk like Migson had been doing here became more insistent.

There were rows of chairs facing the platform, but most of the audience seemed to prefer standing round the walls or at the back where a bar was doing good trade. Moth-eaten curtains in royal-blue velvet were looped up on either side of the platform and a chairman sat on the far side with a glass of gin on the table in front of him and a board above his head, giving the number of the performer on stage.

'Champagne Charlie is my name. Champagne drinking is my game . . .'

A strangled, high tenor voice, a silver-headed cane twirled to indicate devil-may-care, but with a nervous conscientiousness and a quick clutch when the singer nearly dropped it.

'I'm the idol of the barmaids . . .'

Two long steps across the platform, kick on the high notes of 'barmaids'. Not a man at all, but a woman in man's dress. Very popular since the debut of Vesta Tilley but surely dated now and, judging by the small attention given to her by most of the audience, they thought so too. But then the whole place had an old-fashioned feel to it, musty and down-at-heel. Nobody had told Marquesa's that the

101

music hall had gone fashionable these days, with gilt boxes and visits from royalty. So how did Marquesa's get away with charging a pound a head and why had Migson made a journey across London to get here?

Champagne Charlie finished her act and strode off to a final chorus played by the five-piece band sitting below the platform. There was a light scatter of applause, like mice in straw. She was followed by a comedian in costermonger dress whose first joke, about a fisherman, a young woman and a misunderstanding about the length of the pier at Southend, brought a splutter of embarrassed laughter from Freeson, then a nervous glance at me.

'Don't worry, I've heard that one before, only the pier was Blackpool.'

I'd heard most of the others too, though they seemed new to Freeson, which suggested that producers of advanced plays led sheltered lives. While the comedian was reeling them out I looked round, wondering who, if anybody, was likely to answer questions.

It was a mixed audience. The women seemed, on the whole, better dressed than the men, although hardly modish. The tightly corseted, hour-glass figure which, thank the gods, was already fast going out of fashion still reigned at Marquesa's, along with swelling velvet bosoms, skirts with a great frou-frouing of petticoats, picture hats with plumes of ostrich feathers. A rational dress reformer would have despaired. Quite a few were about my height, which made a change from standing out as the tallest woman in a room. The men in comparison seemed shrunken and often furtive looking. A few of the middle-aged ones wore evening dress and kept their top hats on indoors. Then there were the younger ones in velvet smoking jackets with hair sleeked back and covered in oil. Most of those smoked cigarettes or cigarillos and a canopy of blue smoke scented with macassar oil hung just above the level of the gas lamps. When I accidentally backed into one of them and apologised he gave me a venomous look and said nothing. I had the prickly feeling that I was doing something wrong without knowing what.

After the comedian there were a couple of girl dancers,

rather clumsy it seemed to me, but they got enthusiastic yells and wolf-whistles from an audience that was warming up rapidly. Freeson went to the bar and came back with a half-pint of beer and a glass of something fizzy and plum coloured.

'They say the ladies drink port and lemon.'

The lemonade would have been an insult to the port, except that the port was beneath being insulted. I took a sip and looked for somewhere to put it down.

Freeson said: 'Those girls . . .'

'Yes?'

'Oh, nothing.'

He'd cheered up while the comedian was on, but now he seemed ill at ease again.

'Rum sort of place.'

'Very. Can you think why Migson would come all the way out here?'

He shook his head. The girls lurched off stage in a series of high kicks, rather crooked at the knee.

'Ladies and gentlemen . . .'

The chairman was on his feet, obviously working up to one of the big acts. Questioning anybody would have to wait.

'Ladies and gentlemen, may I proudly present the magnificent . . .'

Whistles from the audience.

'. . . the melodious, the apotheosis of female charms . . .'

More whistling and some stamping of feet. This was what they were waiting for.

'Ladies and gentlemen, the amazing Mirabelle Marquesa.'

I hissed to Freeson: 'Have you heard of her?'

He shook his head.

She came running onto the platform in little steps, high-heeled shoes with laces to just below the knee, black and pink skirts caught up at the front to show a froth of pink net petticoats and a glimpse of black stocking below them. A coquettish kick sent the petticoats flying higher, revealing a flash of garter and broad white thigh.

I glanced round me. To my left one of the young men in

a smoking jacket gazed at her like a devotee at an icon, lips slightly apart. To my right, a woman's corseted velvet bosom was heaving with what I took to be envious sighs. Marquesa made a great business of smoothing her skirts down.

'Oops, done it again. You didn't see anything you shouldn't, did you?'

A happy chorus of 'Yes' blasted a cloud of beer and port fumes up to the canopy of tobacco smoke. She gave them a mock frown and patted at her piled-up coiffure of black hair with pink silk roses skewered into it. The last time I'd seen hair like that it was walking round on the end of a horse.

'I'm going to sing you a song about a poor young woman who had a very hard life . . .'

Yells of delight.

'. . . so I do hope you're not going to laugh. Music please, maestro.'

As the band played the introduction, she walked across the stage, swinging her hips, glancing sidelong at the audience. A man in a top hat drained his whisky at a gulp and choked. She began to sing the verse in a throaty contralto.

'Gertie was a good girl,
She came from Southwark way,
Till she met a toff
As she was walking out one day.
Her ma had always told her
To keep away from men . . .'

A shudder on the word 'men', a shaking of white shoulders above the swelling bust. Rather broad white shoulders. I began to see.

I said to Freeson: 'Do you think . . .?'

He was staring as intently as the rest, mouth open.

'But when he took her driving
Well, you know what happened then.'

Anticipatory laughter. A gesture of her hand told them to wait. A large hand in a black net glove.

'I think she's a . . .'

The young man on my left gave me a poisonous look. The music changed rhythm. Her hips swayed like a gate in a gale.

'He went too far –
Well, you knew he would.
She tried to do
What ma said she should.
Shouted "stop" –
Didn't do no good –
Just a little bit too late.'

The audience, overjoyed, roared out the chorus. Marquesa was urging them on from the stage, frothing petticoats, flashing garter.

'She's a man, Mr Freeson.'

The young man in the smoking jacket had his eyes closed, trance-like, and was swaying from side to side. I looked at the woman on my other side but I hadn't needed to look. She was singing the chorus in a healthy baritone. It was that, rather than what I said, that convinced Freeson. He gave one horrified glance at the baritone woman, another at Marquesa on the stage, the next one at me.

'Don't worry, it's not catching.'

His mouth hung open.

'Shall we go?' I said.

I'd found out as much as I needed to and if I didn't get Freeson into the fresh air, he looked liable to faint.

We pushed our way through the crowd and made it to the door while Marquesa was singing the second verse. The same muscular man let us out with a curious glance at Freeson. Goodness knows what he thought I'd been doing to him. In the alleyway he took several deep gulps of air.

'That . . . that woman standing next to you . . . I almost . . . I just happened to brush against her and . . .'

'Don't worry, he probably liked it.'

It didn't seem to console him. As we walked out of the

alleyway we could still hear from behind the closed door
the chorus being belted out by a hundred enthusiastic
voices of all registers:

'. . . shouted "stop" –
Didn't do no good –
Just a little bit too late.'

FIFTEEN

FREESON WAS SILENT FOR MOST of the journey back but kept giving me sidelong looks. We got off at Trafalgar Square, where he gulped a barely civil good night and vanished into what I assumed to be a safely familiar public house. I went towards the Strand and the Crispin Theatre. All the way from the Mile End Road Marquesa's tune had been hammering away in my mind. I knew I'd heard it somewhere recently and yet it wasn't one of those well-known music-hall songs that errand boys whistle.

By the time we'd got to Aldgate I was sure I'd heard it somewhere in the past two days – which meant almost certainly from somebody at the Crispin. Silvester Bonnet was the first name that came to mind, as he'd been on the halls, but somehow I didn't associate the song with him. It had finally hit me as we were going along Cheapside towards St Paul's and the name had been so unexpected that I'd had to bite my tongue to stop myself blurting it out with Freeson sitting beside me.

The front of the Crispin Theatre had a disconsolate look about it. By that time in the evening the audience should have been streaming out, but there were no lights on and the doors were barred. I went down the side street and found that there was at least a light on over the stage door, and a door-keeper on duty inside.

'They've all gone,' he said when he saw me. He sounded quite cheerful about it. 'It says postponed on the posters, but cancelled is what they mean. We're auditioning for a new musical comedy tomorrow.'

He didn't try to hide his relief. Advanced plays meant trouble.

'What about the police?'

'They've gone too, thank God.'

'You've got the addresses of the cast, for forwarding mail?'

At first he thought I was another one wanting to get my lascivious hands on Charles Courts, but when I told him the name I was interested in he gave me the address without fuss.

It was in Bloomsbury. I caught an omnibus and half an hour later was walking down one of the streets of terraced houses that cluster beside the British Museum, and shelter poor scholars and even poorer writers. If London has a Bohemia I suppose Bloomsbury is it, but at eleven o'clock on a November night, with a few street lamps and bare plane trees, it looked as carefree as a frozen dishcloth.

The number where Vincent Colvin lived had half a dozen faded name cards pinned to the flaking paintwork of the front door and the sounds of a tentative guitar coming from behind the ground-floor curtains, with a crack of light showing between them. I knocked on the door but nothing happened. When I knocked a second time the ground-floor window went up and a young man with a snub nose and curly hair looked out. I said I wanted to find Vincent Colvin, he grinned and pointed upstairs, then the window went down again and the guitar returned to its labours. I found that the front door opened with a good push, giving onto a bare hall with a bicycle propped against the wall and a flight of wooden, uncarpeted stairs.

I went up to the first landing by the light of a dim gas lamp. A knock on the first door produced a nervous girl in a dressing gown and the information that Vincent Colvin had the room at the very top. I went up more stairs to a triangular upper landing so narrow that there was just room to stand on it if you kept your feet close together and your elbows against your ribs. The slanting ceiling knocked my hat off and left a line of flaked distemper across it.

At first I thought he must be out. There was no movement inside. Then I saw a newspaper under the door and as I bent to look at it, wondering if he'd been home at all that day, the smell hit me. I shouted his name, banged on the door and when there was no answer threw myself at it. It was a thin, badly fitted door and it rattled on its hinges, but it was bolted and wouldn't give. I called his name again and heard a sound from inside, something between a groan and a drunken man's attempt to speak. I think he might have been trying to ask who was there.

The landing was too small to take a step back. I turned sideways and rammed my shoulder against the door with all my force. I felt the wood and my neck wrench, tried again. This time the wood holding the bolt splintered and I fell into darkness and the smell of gas. I tripped over, feet tangled in the fabric and newspaper he'd used to block the gap under the door. There was no light, no light at all.

I half fell, half stumbled across the small room, finding the window more by accident than anything. The curtains were drawn across it, harsh and heavy. When they fought my effort to pull them aside I yanked them down from their pole. Sash window. It wouldn't move. I cursed and was about to put my fist through a pane when I found a wedge. Once that was gone the sash went up and the air came in, the cold, sooty night air of London but at that point more precious than anything in the Alps. There was a little light too from a street lamp underneath the window, enough to see him lying on a couch. I grabbed him under the arms and dragged him to the open window. He was passive, apart from little groaning sounds that might have been protests.

The gas was still coming, a low roaring sound from somewhere near floor level. I left him propped in a sitting position under the window and found a small gas fire, unlighted but with its tap turned on. I turned it off and the worst of the roaring stopped, but there was still something hissing near my head and something crunching under my feet. I realised that the crunching was the shade from the gas light and the hissing was coming from its pipe, with the mantle taken off. He'd certainly done it thoroughly. I found that switch too and turned it, and the hissing stopped. I could hear footsteps passing in the street underneath the open window, the nervous girl moving about downstairs, the retching of Vincent Colvin as his half-poisoned lungs grabbed for air, whether he liked it or not.

I went over and sat down on the floor beside him.

'It's all right,' I said. 'It will be all right.'

I wondered whether to call a doctor. He needed one, but a doctor would have to report what he found and attempted suicide is a crime. He moved his head towards me but his eyes weren't focusing. The retching became faster, more painful. Then he suddenly rocked forward and was sick all over my shoes. I put my arm round his shoulders, kept his head down.

'That's it. Better out than in.'

Our nurse used to say that, when children's parties had their usual aftermath. Odd the things that come to you. The smell of vomit and brandy added itself to the gas fumes. After that I managed to get him kneeling with his head out of the open window, sucking in air. His breaths were deep and harsh, but sounded more hopeful.

Nobody came. I was glad about that, now that I thought he was going to recover. He showed no sign of throwing himself out of the window, so I left him there while I dragged the couch across to him.

'Can you lie on that?'

'The mess . . .'

'Never mind the mess.'

This time he managed to help a little. I got him lying on the couch beside the window, a cushion under his head.

'Could I have some water?'

I looked round the room, couldn't see any.

'There's a tap . . . on the landing downstairs.'

'You won't move?'

'It's all right. I . . . don't like heights.'

He even managed something like a smile. His sleek black hair was glued to his scalp with sweat. There was a glass with some brandy in it on a table beside where the couch had been. I took it down to the first landing, found a tap and a sink in an alcove, rinsed the glass and filled it with water. While I was doing it the nervous girl looked round her door and asked if anything was wrong. Nothing serious, I said. Mr Colvin had had a bilious turn, but he was getting better. She popped back inside.

When I got back with the water he was half sitting up, leaning on his elbow.

'Did somebody from the theatre send you?'

'Nobody sent me.'

I gave him the water, helping him hold the glass. He drank.

I said: 'You're going to have a terribly big gas bill.'

He looked at me and laughed shakily.

'I wonder how much it costs to kill yourself.'

'You'd never find out, would you? More water?'

He shook his head.

'Have you told anybody downstairs?'

'No. Do you think you could sleep for a while?'

He could. I sat on the floor beside the couch until his breathing was somewhere near normal. Then I cleared up the mess, using the newspaper from under the door. Today's date. So you still buy a newspaper when you're going to kill yourself. I found a floorcloth and a bucket in the alcove on the downstairs landing, swabbed the floor, carried soiled cloth and papers down to the street. The man on the ground floor was still negotiating with his guitar. A policeman paced past on his beat. Back in the room I replaced the gas mantle on its burner but decided against lighting it. Fresh air was winning the battle but it still wasn't safe to strike matches.

I found a blanket and put it over Vincent, then, in coat and gloves against the cold air from the window, settled myself in the room's one armchair and watched him while he slept.

Migson had a ticket for Marquesa's. Vincent Colvin, the first day I met him, had hummed Marquesa's tune. Migson was dead and Colvin had tried to kill himself. When I looked at it like that I had to ask myself whether I'd done Colvin a favour after all.

It was at about half-past five in the morning, as the milk cart came on its rounds in the dimly lit street beneath us, that he began to stir. There was a white frost on the pavement by then and it was freezing cold in the room

111

because I hadn't dared close the window. I must have dozed myself, because I was suddenly conscious that he was looking at me and that he'd recovered. His expression was the cynical one I'd noticed that first day at the threatre, as if it were all a joke, but an old one.

'May I offer you some coffee, Miss Bray?'

'Yes please.'

He got up slowly, draping the blanket round his shoulders like a cloak. There was even a kind of elegance about it. It was still dark, apart from the street lamp. His eyes went to the gas burner with the mantle back in place but no shade, to the matches on the table. As if rehearsing a play that wasn't yet familiar he picked up the matches and, with the smallest of hesitations, turned on the gas and lit it. Nicely done. I closed the window.

Moving slowly still, but steadily, he went to a cupboard in the corner and took out a spirit stove, a tin of coffee beans, a grinder. The noise when he turned the grinder handle was the loudest thing I'd heard since I burst in through the door. I must have jumped.

'I'm sorry. Did I scare you?'

A touch of irony in his smile. It was good coffee, hot and black. We drank it without speaking, me in the armchair, he walking stiffly round the room. I put down my empty cup.

'More?'

'No thank you.'

'Well then . . .'

He crossed to the couch by the window, still as if obeying a stage direction, sat down, crossed one knee over the other.

'. . . let battle commence.'

He was still weak, but it was no time for chivalry.

'Did you meet Migson at Marquesa's?'

He'd expected that.

'Yes. As a matter of interest, how did you know? Did the police tell you?'

'I don't think the police know about it. There was a ticket that fell out of his things. I went there last night and recognised a song I'd heard you whistling.'

112

'Did you enjoy yourself?'

'It came as something of a surprise.'

'You hadn't encountered transvestites before?'

I went through the Latin roots and got there.

'Is that what they're called? No, I don't think I had.'

Though, come to think of it, there were a few of my aunt's friends I'd have my doubts about from now on.

'In case it interests you, I'm not one. But there are . . . circles that overlap. One of the places where they overlap is Marquesa's.'

'You're not, but Migson was?'

'As you say, Migson was.'

'Was he a friend of yours?'

'Certainly not. I disliked the man. Until he walked into the rehearsal three days ago I'd only met him twice, both times at Marquesa's in the company of other people.'

'Did you know he worked at the Lord Chamberlain's department?'

'No. Perhaps I should have guessed.'

'When was the last time you met him at Marquesa's?'

'About two weeks ago. It was just after we started rehearsals on the *Cinderella* piece.'

'Did you talk about that?'

'We all did. It was a theatrical crowd. But yes, Migson was very curious about it.'

'Did that seem strange to you?'

He shook his head.

'Oh no, London's full of people like him, little stage-struck people who cling round anything that's got the smell of greasepaint about it.'

'So it was a shock to you when he arrived at the Crispin claiming to be the Lord Chamberlain's representative?'

'Yes.'

He went over to the table and poured himself another half-cup of coffee, although it must have been going cold. His hand shook a very little.

'You said "claiming to be". Does that mean he wasn't?'

I told him about Migson's ambiguous status. He listened and nodded.

'That explains a lot.'

'What?'

'His chance to be in a theatre for a few days, backstage with the cast.'

'Only that?'

He didn't answer. I let him swallow a good gulp of coffee before my next question.

'Was Migson blackmailing you?'

He gave me a straight look and shook his head slowly.

'No.'

'Did you kill him?'

'No.'

'Then why did you try to kill yourself?'

He shrugged, then a long pause before he answered.

'When something like this happens, a lot of other things come pouring out, whether they have anything to do with it or not. I could tell when that police inspector spoke to me that he knew, or sensed, something about me.'

'Would that matter, if your private life had nothing to do with why he was murdered?'

'As far as the law's concerned, we have no private life. You saw what they did to Wilde.'

'That was barbarous.'

Another shrug.

'It happened.'

'And because of this fear of what might come out, you decided to kill yourself?'

The cup, empty, dangled from his fingers.

'Sometimes you feel . . . you feel so damned weary that you ask yourself whether it's worth all the trouble. When you're in that mood perhaps it takes just one thing more and . . .'

His voice trailed away. He gave an annoyed shake of the shoulders.

'But you say Migson wasn't blackmailing you?'

'He wasn't. I doubt if he knew enough about me in any case. Besides, I wasn't the fish he was after.'

'Who was?'

He'd been looking at the floor, but when I said this his eyes came back to my face.

'What's your interest in this? Are you going to tell the

inspector all about it?'

'My interest is finding out who killed Migson. I shan't tell the inspector about this unless I have to, no.'

'Why bother about the wretched man?'

'Suppose the wrong person is blamed?'

'We're all of us blamed for the wrong things and never forgiven for the right ones.'

'Oscar?'

'A long way after. I need more coffee.'

I watched him making it. It was still dark outside but there was more traffic in the street on hooves and wheels, and the feel of the house coming to life as people began to stir downstairs. The room was perishing cold. He sat down, waiting for the coffee to brew.

'Did you talk to Migson after he arrived at the theatre?'

'No. I kept well clear of him.'

'You weren't on your own with him at all?'

'Only once, and that wasn't alone exactly.'

'Tell me about it.'

He waited till the coffee was poured.

'You remember that scene where we had the trouble from the audience? Silvester Bonnet and I were the last two off stage.'

I thought back, and he was right. Cinderella went first, then Prince Charming, leaving Dandini to exchange a few words with Buttons.

'I came off the stage bursting to go to the lavatory, never mind what was going on in the auditorium.'

Both the men's and women's lavatories, I remembered, were down a side corridor before you got to the dressing rooms as you came off stage.

'I went in there in a hurry. I was doing what I'd come in to do when I realised I wasn't on my own. There are two cubicles at the end and I heard voices coming from them, two people talking to each other. One of the voices was Migson's. I was still standing there when he came rushing past me.'

I hardly dared to breathe. If this was right, Migson at that point couldn't have had as much as ten minutes to live. I waited for Vincent Colvin to go on, but had to

115

prompt him.

'What was Migson wearing?'

'Bella Flanagan's costume. The blue leather and fur, and the hat.'

'Did he say anything to you?'

'No. He just looked at me and ran out. He was in a bad state, nearly crying.'

'And he'd been talking to somebody in the next cubicle. Somebody whose voice you recognised?'

'Yes.'

'Whose?'

A moment's hesitation.

'Charles Courts'.'

He didn't look at me. He'd said the name flatly, without like or dislike in it.

'What were they talking about?'

'Charles was telling him to go away, out of the theatre. Migson kept saying he wasn't doing any harm.'

'Did Charles sound angry?'

'Yes.'

'Did you speak to Charles?'

'No. When I went out he was still in the cubicle. I'm sure he didn't know I was there.'

'What about Migson?'

'By the time I'd adjusted my dress and gone outside there was no sign of him.'

'What did you do then?'

'Went to my dressing room. I stayed there till the five-minute call.'

'And you're quite certain it was Charles' voice you heard in the lavatory?'

'Yes. We'd been rehearsing together for two weeks, remember.'

'What do you think of Charles?'

'Character or talent?'

'Both.'

'He's competent. I've no strong feelings about him. Pleasant enough, easy to work with. Different worlds.'

Down below a door slammed. A whiff of warm bread came up from the frosty street as a baker's van passed.

116

'Well, Miss Bray, what are you going to do about it?'

'I wish I knew.'

There'd never been much colour in his face, but there was more life about him now. I decided it would be safe to leave him.

'You're not going to try it again, are you?'

He gave me a lopsided smile.

'No, not this time. I must accept the verdict of the gods, I suppose, even if it means no more dividends for the gas-company shareholders.'

He came with me downstairs and held open the front door. It was just getting light. As I went down the steps he stood in the doorway and raised a hand to me.

'Good hunting . . .'

Then, after a well-timed pause, '. . . I think.'

SIXTEEN

I'D BEEN HALF SICK WITH tiredness, but the frosty air woke me enough to make me consider Vincent Colvin's question of what I was going to do. Home and bed beckoned, but so did the need to know how far the police had got in their investigations. It was too early to go to the theatre, so, knowing that Shaw was an early riser, I walked across High Holborn and dodged through the cabbage carts at Covent Garden to his flat in Adelphi Terrace. His secretary, Judy, answered the door, looking strained.

'There's a police inspector with him.'

She was trying very hard to stay calm about it.

'Does he look like a frog?'

'That's the one.'

'When did he get here?'

'Ten minutes ago. He said he wanted to speak to Mr Shaw urgently.'

I said I thought I should join them and she showed me into the study. Shaw was at his desk, a stack of mail in front of him. Inspector Merit was sitting awkwardly on an easy chair, hat and gloves balanced on his knee. Shaw seemed pleased to see me.

'Good morning, Nell. I'm just confessing to the inspector that I murdered Matthew Migson in retaliation for what the Lord Chamberlain's done to my plays.'

The inspector smiled a nervous smile.

'One of Mr Shaw's jokes, of course.'

'Not in the least. Since he was a court official it may amount to treason as well as murder. Will you come and see me, Nell, when I'm executed on Tower Hill?'

I said I'd do my best to push my way through the

118

cheering crowds. It was clear that Shaw was worried.

The inspector gave me a pleading look.

'I was asking Mr Shaw if he happened to know the whereabouts of Mr Charles Courts.'

'And I was explaining to the inspector that Mr Courts' whereabouts are his own concern.'

In view of what I'd just heard from Vincent Colvin, this was disturbing news.

'In all seriousness, Mr Shaw, if you know where Mr Courts is, you have a duty to tell me.'

'If I knew, I'm not convinced that I should have any such duty. As it is, I'm spared the dilemma because I don't know.'

The inspector turned his weary eyes on me.

'What about you, Miss Bray?'

'I've no idea. I parted company with him yesterday morning, not long after he'd paid his fine at Marlborough Street police court.'

'Where was it you last saw him?'

'Marble Arch.'

'And you don't know where he was going after that?'

'No.'

Shaw was looking alarmed. He would have no way of knowing about Charles' exhibition outside Lord Penwardine's house. The inspector, though, would have been informed about it.

'Was he going back to his flat?'

'I don't know. I don't even know where his flat is.'

'Maida Vale. One of my men went there early this morning. He wasn't there. His housekeeper says he didn't come in last night.'

He stared sorrowfully from one to the other of us, as if we could produce Charles if we really tried.

Shaw said: 'Why do you want him in any case? You questioned him at the same time as the rest of us.'

'There have been . . . certain developments since then.'

He expected us to ask. Shaw left it to me.

'What developments?'

The inspector shifted in his chair.

'Was either of you aware that Mr Courts had a prior acquaintanceship with Mr Migson?'

119

'Inspector, I was concerned only with his acting abilities, not his social diary.'

'So the answer is no?'

'The answer is no.'

He turned to me. I hedged.

'Before Migson arrived at the dress rehearsal, you mean?'

A nod. I chose my tense carefully.

'As far as I knew, that was the first time they'd set eyes on each other.'

He shook his head.

'In the light of what we know now, that's highly unlikely.'

I thought he meant my answer was unlikely, but luckily said nothing and let him go on.

'Cambridge colleges, so I understand, are not very large places. It's unlikely that two young gentlemen could have attended one for two years at the same time without meeting each other.'

This came as a shock, and not from the direction I'd expected.

'Charles Courts and Matthew Migson were at college together?'

He nodded.

'So far we've been able to find out surprisingly little about Mr Migson's background. But of course the Lord Chamberlain's department kept a copy of the letter he wrote when he applied for his position. A college was mentioned. We made enquiries at the college and Matthew Migson did indeed attend it for three years. Mr Courts was a year senior to him, which means, I take it, that he was there for two of those three years.'

We said nothing.

'That surprises you, Miss Bray?'

Why was he concentrating on me? I tried to wipe any expression off my face and said, truthfully, that it did. I wondered if he knew about Marquesa's yet, or the argument in the lavatory. Probably not, or he'd have asked about them.

'So you will understand why we are anxious to speak to

Mr Courts again. We'd like to know, among other things, why he didn't mention this to us.'

So should I, I thought. I was glad, like Shaw, that I honestly didn't know where Charles might be found.

The inspector fidgeted with his hat and gloves and gazed from Shaw to me with his sad frog eyes. After a long silence he stood up and apologised to Shaw for interrupting him.

'If either of you decide you can help me, you'll find me at Scotland Yard, just around the corner.'

We heard Judy showing him out. Shaw and I stared at each other.

'What are you going to do about Bella, Nell?'

'Why me?'

'You're supposed to be looking after her.'

'I rather thought her husband was doing that now.'

It came as a jolt to him. I'd wrongly assumed that he knew, since everybody else seemed to, about Bella's return to the marital home. I found out later from Judy that he'd plunged into feverish work all the previous day, trying to forget about Migson's death. Now he knew it wouldn't go away.

'Why did she do that?'

'I don't know.'

'Somebody will have to warn her.'

'About the police wanting to speak to Charles?'

I noticed he'd said 'warn'.

'Did Charles Courts kill that man?'

I didn't answer. I was wondering whether to tell him about Marquesa's, and Vincent Colvin's attempt to kill himself. The scales came down against it. He had one of the clearest minds I'd ever encountered but it had its blind spots. Marquesa's would worry him because he wouldn't understand it, and I thought I'd given at least half a promise to Vincent.

'Oh, confound them all. I have work to do. We all have work to do. Finding out who killed the wretched man won't bring him back to life again. Quite the contrary, it will make somebody else dead.'

We stared at each other. Having summoned up that

thought, he tried to drive it away with flippancy like a fly swatter.

'They can't hang Charles. He's by no means a bad actor, if you make allowances for his looks. I'll draw up a list of half a dozen actors they're welcome to hang instead.'

'Will Vincent Colvin be on it?'

'Certainly not. He's a much more versatile actor than Charles.'

'Do you know him well?'

'He's acted in three plays of mine. He's one of the most intelligent actors I've met.'

No, I wouldn't tell him about last night.

I stood up. When he asked me where I was going I said home, I supposed.

'Will you be going past the Crispin Theatre? I want to leave something there for Sylvia Bonnet.'

I said I'd take it. The envelope he gave me felt as if it had banknotes inside.

'Tell them to make sure it goes to Sylvia, not Silvester. She's a good, hard-working woman. It's not her fault if she can't stop her husband drinking.'

It was typical of him to be generous and embarrassed about it. When Judy let me out she seemed relieved that neither of us had been arrested yet.

The Crispin was transformed. With Shaw's cast in residence there'd been a purposeful, almost intellectual feel about it. Now with auditions going on for something called, I think, *Minnesota Minny*, it was like a circus crossed with a refugee camp. A line of terriers and their owners waited outside the stage door to audition, as I later discovered, for the key role of the hero's dog. The stage door-keeper was assuring a large man in buckskins that they weren't taking the lariat spinners until after lunch while fielding a couple of terriers trying to jump the queue. He looked a lot happier than when I'd last seen him. When I tried to leave the envelope for Sylvia he told me I'd find her on stage.

'She's going for Minny's mother.'

I took the familiar path along the dressing-room corridor to the back of the stage. All the *Cinderella* scenery and the balloon had gone, leaving a barn-like space that dwarfed the group of women standing in the wings. Sylvia was one of the women. When she saw me she waved and put a finger to her lips. I took that as a sign to wait and keep quiet and stood there while three actresses went through their audition songs with the backing of a bored pianist. Sylvia followed them and seemed to me far and away the best, but she only got a curt 'Thank you, we'll let you know' from a shadowy figure in the stalls. She came over to me, hitching on her coat and rolling up her music.

'Well, that's done. Did you want to see me?'

'Mr Shaw asked me to give you this.'

An odd expression went across her face when she felt the banknotes, part relief, part shame.

'He didn't have to. We'd been paid for the week.'

'Don't worry. He can afford it.'

'You look as worn out as I feel. Would you like to come in for coffee? We live just up St Martin's Lane.'

Their digs were in one of the little alleys between St Martin's Lane and Charing Cross Road, above a theatrical costumiers. The combined living room and kitchen was neat but bleak, hardly warmer than the air outside. She knelt to put a match to the fire.

'I didn't bother to light it before we went out this morning, and Silvester probably won't be back till late.'

The coffee was hot and milky. She slipped out for a few minutes and came back with a bag of sticky buns, warm from the bakery.

'Do you think you'll get the part?'

'Oh, chorus and understudy for me, I expect. There's a comedy saloon-bar keeper Silvester might get if he stays sober.'

We sat companionably by the fire, drinking coffee and eating buns.

I said experimentally: 'I've been talking to Vincent Colvin.'

'Oh yes. How is he?'

Her voice was non-committal.

'Depressed by it all. We were talking about what happened in that long interval. He stayed in his dressing

123

room all the time.'

She said at once: 'So did we, in Silvester's at any rate. I knew as soon as he came off stage that it would be a while before we got started again, if we ever did, and I didn't want him deciding there was time to nip off to the pub. So I was waiting for him in his dressing room, locked the door behind him when he came in and put the key in my pocket.'

'Was he annoyed?'

'He pretended to be at first.'

'And you both stayed in there the whole time?'

'Yes. We thought it was a toss-up whether they'd go on with the play or not, so we might as well make ourselves comfortable while they sorted it out. Once Silvester had finished acting annoyed, that is.'

She smiled to herself, as if the memory of being locked in a dressing room with her husband wasn't so bad.

'We told the inspector we were playing cards. That wasn't quite the game, but near enough.'

Heavy steps came hurrying up the stairs. Sylvia was on her feet. The door flew open and there was Silvester Bonnet, in hat, scarf and overcoat, bringing a blast of cold air with him.

'Sylvia, love, we don't have to worry. They let him go yesterday, so that's all right.'

SEVENTEEN

WHEN HE SAW I WAS there he changed scene instantly.

'Dear lady, excuse me. I didn't see you.'

He bowed dramatically and kissed my hand. Sylvia giggled: 'Oh, you fool.'

But it was a nervous giggle and she glanced sideways at me to see how I was taking it.

'Buns! Were you keeping them all for yourself, you greedy hussy?'

He fell on the two that were left, one in each hand, took a bite from each, rounded eyes beaming stage voracity. Sylvia ran to him and punched his chest, but softly. Altogether a picture of married bliss, although I noticed that she'd managed to hide the envelope with the banknotes as soon as he came in.

She giggled: 'You've been drinking.'

'A modest half only, my dearest. Certain false friends tried to persuade me to stay for another. I refused. I told them if they wished to wallow in swinish drunkenness they'd have to do it without the benefit of my company because I had the sweetest little wife in the world waiting for me at home.'

I said, breaking up the touching scene: 'And who exactly did they let go yesterday?'

He tried to pass over it, wrinkling his forehead and chewing bun as if he didn't know what I was talking about. But all the pretence of gaiety went out of Sylvia. She sighed and sat down heavily on a chair by the fire.

'You'd better tell her. Miss Bray knows about these things better than we do. She'll advise us.'

'There's nothing to advise about. I told you, they let him

out yesterday morning. They wouldn't have done that if he'd killed the poor blighter, would they?'

I said: 'I gather we're talking about Piggy Ditchbrake.'

I'd kept my eyes on Sylvia and she nodded. Silvester said nothing. He was still standing there in scarf and overcoat.

'I really think you'd better tell me.'

'There's not a lot to tell.'

But his voice had gone quiet and depressed. He drew a wooden chair out from the table, sat on it and took a deep breath.

'What do you know about this Piggy Ditchbrake?'

I said: 'That he's a great friend of Bella's husband, Lord Penwardine. That he stirred up most of the trouble on opening night. That he was found backstage after Migson had been murdered.'

'Well you see, Miss Bray, I couldn't know any of that, could I? Not when I first met him.'

'When and where was that?'

Sylvia said, wearily: 'In a public house. Where else?'

Silvester gave her a reproachful look.

'It was, as my wife says, in a public hostelry across the road from the Crispin. As to when, it was a few days after we started rehearsals, about two weeks ago.'

'What happened?'

'Well, nothing happened as such. That is . . .'

Sylvia's voice cut in, low but decisive.

'You'd better tell her what you did.'

His voice rose in a plaintive appeal.

'What I did? From the way you go on about it, you'd think I'd sold half the Royal Navy to the Kaiser. He only wanted a loan of my script, for goodness sake.'

'Piggy Ditchbrake asked you for a loan of your *Cinderella* script two weeks ago? How did he know about it?'

Silvester looked towards his wife, but got no help.

'There's been quite a bit about it in the papers, because of Lady Penwardine. We happened to get talking in the pub, and he knew I was in the production because of something the landlord said. He told me how much he admired the work of George Bernard Shaw . . .'

'A man like Piggy Ditchbrake. Didn't that surprise you?'

126

'Why should it? It takes all sorts. If he wanted to borrow it for a read over the weekend, it was no skin off my nose.'

'Did he pay you?'

'A few pounds may have changed hands. Comes in useful, you know, for tipping your footmen.'

He mimed a lordly handing-out of largesse. Sylvia's eyes went to her bag on the table.

'I suppose you thought he was going to pirate it abroad,' I said.

From the corner of my eye I saw Sylvia nod. Silvester said nothing, but I knew from his silence I'd guessed right. My translation work had taught me something about the problems of literary piracy.

'When did you realise that wasn't what he'd wanted it for, after all?'

He said, very subdued now: 'Only when they started shouting things from the audience.'

'Piggy had returned the script by then, of course.'

'Oh yes, in the public house on the Monday morning after I gave it to him, as agreed. I didn't see him again until I had cause to rescue you from his unwanted attentions outside the theatre on opening night.'

'Yes, I had an idea you'd recognised him.'

'I didn't let on, because I thought I might have done the wrong thing. Still, it was spilt milk by then.'

'I suppose you didn't tell the inspector about this.'

'No.'

None of us said anything for a while. Then Sylvia asked quietly:

'Will you have to tell Mr Shaw about this? He's always been good to us.'

'Not if I can help it. But none of this accounts for why Silvester was so relieved when he found out the police had released Piggy.'

'Well, if they hadn't, I might have had to tell them about seeing him backstage not long after the Migson man was shot. Then they'd have wanted to know how I recognised him and it would all have come out.'

'When exactly did you see him backstage?'

'Just before we started up again, after the trouble. We'd

127

had the five-minute call, so her ladyship here had to unlock my dressing-room door and let me out. I was going along the corridor and he came out of one of the empty dressing rooms and nearly bumped into me. I said, "You're not supposed to be in here, Piggy" and he mumbled something about looking for somebody. I wasn't feeling any too pleased with him by then, but I couldn't stay there arguing because I was wanted on stage, so I went off and left him there. That was the last I saw of him before the police found him.'

By that point, Migson had probably been dead for about fifteen minutes.

'Was Piggy still wearing his outdoor clothes?'

'His overcoat, yes. I don't remember a hat.'

'Did you ask him who he was looking for?'

'I didn't have time. Anyway, I thought I could guess.'

'Who?'

'The one who started all the trouble in the first place.'

Sylvia began wearily: 'You can't say it was all her fault . . .'

'Well, I can. The aristocracy should have enough room in their own homes to sort out their problems, without doing it all over our stage.'

'So you thought Piggy was looking for Bella Flanagan?'

'That's the one, yes.'

'He must have come in by the stage door when it was left unguarded. You know we'd thrown him out?'

'I know now. I didn't know at the time.'

He moved suddenly and sprawled on the rag rug in front of the fire, his head level with his wife's knees.

'So you see, Miss Bray, there's no point in telling the inspector all this and making trouble for myself if he had nothing to do with the murder, is there?'

Then, as if drawing a line under it all, he looked up at Sylvia, took her hand and smiled.

'Now, forgive your poor old husband and tell me how you did at the audition.'

'Oh, all right, but that Brummie cow will get it as usual. I told you that as soon as we knew who the producer was and . . .'

I said goodbye and left them to it, closing the door behind me. So Bella had been right in thinking there was a spy, wrong in suspecting Migson, on that score at any rate. Tiredness had set in with a vengeance by now. I wanted home and bed. To get to the underground railway station at Charing Cross I had to pass the turning leading to the Crispin Theatre. On the corner I saw a familiar face, eyes bulging under the brim of a very black bowler hat. I tried to dodge but he saw me.

'Hello again, Miss Bray. I've just been to the theatre to see if Mr Courts looked in there this morning. I gather the answer is no.'

'That's not surprising, inspector. It's a different play now.'

'So it seems. But the stage hands are the same.'

The look in his eyes gave an edge to the words. His manner was several degrees colder than in Shaw's study.

'One of the stage hands has just told us something we should have known about thirty-six hours ago. Something you knew about, Miss Bray, as well as all the rest of you at the dress rehearsal.'

'Oh? What was that?'

But I knew.

'I assume you were there when Mr Courts attacked Mr Migson?'

'I'd hardly call it an attack. It was a dress rehearsal. People were naturally tense.'

'I don't know a lot about the theatre, Miss Bray. Is it customary for actors to slap public officials at dress rehearsals?'

I said nothing. He waited.

'And you don't know where Mr Courts is now?'

'I've already told you so.'

'I'm asking you again because if you did know it would be a very serious offence now not to tell me.'

'Would it?'

'Yes. A warrant is now out for the arrest of Mr Charles Courts on a charge of murdering Mr Matthew Migson.'

He held his stare for a pause of five seconds, then walked slowly away. An actor couldn't have timed it better.

129

EIGHTEEN

I WENT HOME. I DIDN'T know what else to do. I was tired to the bone and wanted to go to sleep and wake up when it was all over. On the Underground to Hampstead I kept dozing off and waking when I slumped against the shoulder of the woman next to me, with Bella and Charles always the first things on my mind.

At home, although I'd only been away for the space of three postal deliveries, there was a mountain of mail on the mat and the cats were staging a protest on top of the kitchen table. I dumped the mail on my desk without looking at it, found some boiled fish for the cats and made myself a cup of tea while they ate. After that, as usual, they wanted a walk in the lane outside. I opened the back gate for them and walked to the end of the lane and back again, trying not to think. The evidence against Charles, though far from conclusive, was building up fast. That made Bella's behaviour all the more disturbing. I wondered if the inspector knew that she'd been away from her dressing room in that long interval.

It was still just after midday, with a pale sun trying to drive away the frost. I left it to get on with it and went inside, leaving the back door a few inches ajar so that the cats could come in. I undressed down to my underwear, slid under the sheets and sleep hit me like a sledge hammer. It was quite dark when I woke up, but at that time of year it gets dark early and the sounds of traffic from Heath Street told me that it wasn't late. I lit the candle on the bedside table, not bothering with the gas, and saw it was just past five. Afternoon, not morning, from the sounds.

With the guilty feeling that comes to you when you've slept during the day I went downstairs, still carrying the candle, intent on tea and hunks of bread and Cheshire cheese. A cat wrapped itself round my shins on the stairs and I warned it to be careful. I was still feeling fragile. I'd like to be able to say that I had a sixth sense that there was somebody else in the house but I had none at all, not until I'd gone through the dark living room and had put the candle down on the kitchen table, looking for the matches to light the gas.

'Please. Please can we talk?'

A small breathless voice. A voice I'd heard before, although once only. I nearly yelled, but bit my tongue. I'd got the matchbox in my hand by then and I could feel the wood splintering as I gripped it. I froze and made myself think. She was somewhere near the back door. I could make out a smudge of pale face, but she was wearing a dark coat and the face was all I could see. I turned the gas on and held a match to the mantle. I didn't turn until the glow from it had spread out to fill the room, then I looked at her. The finch-like mouth was still gaping from its question. Her grey eyes were huge and a little mad looking, the blonde hair frizzing out from under her fur hat like frosted grass.

'How did you get in?'

'You . . . you left the back door open. I . . . I followed you from the theatre this morning.'

She took sharp little gasps of air between the words, as if she'd been running, but her chilled look showed she'd been waiting for some time.

'Have you been here all the time I was asleep?'

She nodded.

'I . . . I didn't want to disturb you.'

'Standing out here in the kitchen?'

'I sat . . . on the chair . . . for most of the time.'

This was becoming ridiculous. I was on the verge of apologising to her for not making her more comfortable. Goodness knows how she did it. It might have been the slight lisp in the voice, or the sharp urgency of that little mouth.

'We'd better go through to the other room.'

131

I sat her down in an armchair and she watched while I lit the fire. It was only seventy hours or so since Bella had sat in the same chair and watched me, and it was probably just as well that this young woman didn't know that. I'd no doubt at all why she'd come here. It was part of her crazed pursuit of Charles Courts, like the only other time I'd seen her when she was conquering her nerves to try to get his address from the stage door-keeper. She must have been haunting the theatre again this morning and recognised me then, presumably following me all the way to the Bonnets' lodgings and waiting while I was inside. If I hadn't been so tired and worried I'd surely have spotted her. She'd shown, I had to admit, immense patience and determination. I only wished she were using them in a better cause than pursuing some actor who'd probably never set eyes on her in his life.

When the fire was going I settled in the chair opposite her.

'For a start, I don't even know your name.'

A little gasp.

'Penelope. Penelope Brown.'

The faithful Penelope. I didn't believe her for a moment, but since all I intended to do was give her some good advice and send her on her way, that didn't matter.

'Well, Penelope Brown, what is all this about?'

She took two deep breaths. Her hands, in their brown gloves, were locked together.

'I wanted to talk to you because you're a friend of Lady Penwardine. I saw you with her.'

'Well?'

I owed her no explanation of how brief my friendship with Bella had been so far.

'I thought . . . thought you might . . .'

She must have seen the impatience in my face because she took a grip on herself and began talking faster and more coherently.

'I thought you might talk to her, persuade her to let him go. She doesn't love him, not like I do. She doesn't need him, she's got another man, probably more than one if the truth be known. She should leave him for me. I love him, you see. I always shall, whatever happens.'

I found myself creasing the skin of my forehead with my fingers, the way I'd seen the inspector do. It didn't help. I still had the urge to pick her up by the scruff of her little neck, bundle her across the road to Whitestone pond and dunk some sense into her. If this was the effect Charles Courts had on women, then perhaps prison was the best place for him. I wondered if it would drive the nonsense out of her if I told her her hero was being hunted by the police on a murder charge, but decided it would probably make things worse. She'd want to share the condemned cell with him.

'Hasn't it struck you,' I said, 'that this isn't very dignified?'

'I've tried being dignified. It's done no good, no good at all. It won't while she's there.'

'Look, even if I had any influence over Lady Penwardine, and I can assure you I haven't, I shouldn't dream of using it in the way you want. If there's one thing a human being should be allowed to decide for him or herself, it's surely the choice of partners.'

'He wasn't given a choice. She practically threw herself at him.'

'The world's full of men. I'm sure if you put all this energy into looking around, you'd find one quite suitable.'

To my embarrassment, her eyes began to fill up with tears.

'You don't understand. I want his son. He wants me to have his son.'

'Penelope, or whatever your name is, please stop this. It's hysteria.'

But she was beyond stopping. Tears ran down her cheeks. Her voice broke into a wail.

'Even his mother wants me to have his son.'

This beat everything. I had grave doubts that she'd ever met Charles, let alone his mother. She sobbed for a while, dabbing at her eyes with a lace-edged handkerchief, but stopped when she realised that I had no intention of comforting her. I knew that if I laid a hand on her I'd probably end up shaking her until her teeth rattled. After

133

a last dab she raised her head and gave me a hard look from her damp grey eyes.

'So you won't help me?'

'I will help you by advising you to get this man out of your head and do something useful with your life.'

'But I can't. He is my life. We were meant for each other. We always were.'

I breathed long and deeply. She stared at me, as if she hoped I'd change my mind.

'In that case, I can't help you. Now, if you'd kindly go, I've plenty of work to get on with.'

Her eyes, her whole body went hard. I knew I'd made an enemy, but at that point it was the least of my worries. I never expected to see her again.

'I see,' she said. 'I should have known you'd be on her side.'

I opened the back door and the fire flickered in the rush of cold air.

'You came in that way, so you'd better go out that way. Good evening.'

She went. I stood at the door and watched until the gate slammed behind her, then listened to her steps along the hard earth of the lane. When they'd faded away I shut the door and went inside.

'Damn all handsome men,' I said to the cats.

They purred.

'And double damn all silly women.'

I turned for relief to the pile of mail on my desk, sorting it into urgent, less urgent and shouldn't-be-wasting-my-time. The postcard was only a small one and I didn't even notice it until I picked up the less urgent heap to put it in a tray, then it slid out at me. This time it wasn't from George Bernard Shaw. The address was in handwriting that was educated but unfamiliar to me, the postmark showed it had been posted in Reading the evening before.

The message on the other side was simple:

Miss Bray, Would you please be kind enough to meet me outside Reading Station at eight o'clock on Saturday morning. Please tell nobody else about this.

Saturday was the following day. There was no address on the card. The signature was Charles Courts'.

NINETEEN

THERE WERE THREE THINGS I could do. I could take the postcard to the inspector at once. I could burn it and forget it had existed. Or I could do as Charles Courts asked. The first was ruled out by the same instinct that would stop me from telling a huntsman which way a fox had run. I might have overcome that instinct if I'd trusted the inspector more, but he'd refused to accept my evidence that Lord Penwardine had been near the theatre on the evening of the murder and had been quick to release Piggy Ditchbrake. That left the other two options, so I used my own way of throwing the dice. I decided that if I woke up by six o'clock the next morning, in time to keep the appointment at Reading at eight, I'd meet Charles. If not, the card would go on the fire.

The dice were loaded, of course. I'd slept during the day, so naturally there was no chance of sleeping a long night. When I woke up, the dark and silence of very early morning were still over everything. I dressed by candlelight in the tweed skirt, jacket and boots I keep for serious walking, not knowing how the day would turn out. Fed the cats, quick breakfast of coffee, bread and gooseberry jam, then a walk through sleeping Hampstead in the dark and frosty morning to catch the tram from the top of Haverstock Hill. The odd, hollow feeling inside was from being up so early. Nothing to do, of course, with going to meet a man who might be a murderer.

It was dark for the whole train journey from Paddington to Reading, apart from a few lamps on railway-station platforms and clusters of lights in towns beginning to wake up along the way. Even in the carriage it was cold. As we came to Reading there was just enough daylight to show a gleam of the Thames, pale pewter colour and as cold as a fish's belly. I was outside the station at five mintues to the hour, waiting among the farm carts delivering crates of vegetables and bundles of dead pheasants and rabbits for loading onto trains. Almost at once two headlamps began to move towards me from further along the station yard and a motor car came weaving slowly in among the carts. The figure at the wheel was wearing cap and goggles, the collar of his heavy coat turned up.

'Thank you for coming, Miss Bray. Could you let yourself in? I don't want to switch the engine off.'

He had to shout to make himself heard above it. I opened the door and climbed in beside him.

'There are some goggles for you under the seat.'

'Do you know there's a warrant out for your arrest?'

I knew the engine was making too much noise for the men with the farm carts to hear me.

'What for?'

'Murdering Migson.'

'Oh.'

That was all. He manoeuvred us round and out of the station yard. There were a few streaks of sunrise in the sky now, the colour of uncooked bacon. I didn't need to ask what he was doing there. Lord Penwardine's country estate in the Vale of the White Horse should be less than two hours drive away from Reading. When we were well clear of the town he stopped the motor car in a field gateway between bare elm hedges. It was more light that dark now. Every twig was outlined with frost and cows shifted their feet on hard earth on the other side of the gate. It was very quiet with the engine switched off, apart from a blackbird protesting at the invasion of its territory.

'Do the police know where I am?'

'They didn't yesterday. I haven't told them about your card. But don't you think it would be best if you . . . arranged to meet them?'

'Let them arrest me, you mean?'

'Yes.'

'Not before I've spoken to Bella.'

His gloved hands closed tightly round the steering wheel.

'I suppose that's why you've come down here, to try to see her.'

'Yes.'

'It won't be any easier than in London.'

'It will – the way I'm going to do it.'

His face was white and pinched, as if he hadn't slept. Apart from the change of clothes he looked even worse than in the police court.

'It was good of you to come. Even if she won't speak to me, she might speak to you.'

'We'd have to get to her first.'

'Will you do that for me? At least try to get her to talk to me?'

'I can't drag her out for you if she won't come.'

We sat there for a while. I listened to the blackbird. Charles seemed to be trying to absorb what I'd told him.

'Why do they think I killed him?'

'They heard what happened between the two of you at rehearsal. They'd already found out you were at the same college at Cambridge. Inspector Merit thinks it's suspicious that you didn't tell them about it.'

'I suppose I was too embarrassed.'

He seemed surprised at his own weakness.

'You mean, about Marquesa's and so on?'

'Marquesa's? Who or what is Marquesa's?'

He sounded puzzled, but then he would.

'It's an old-fashioned music hall in the East End where transvestites go.'

'Trans . . .?'

I could see he was making the same trip to Latin roots. When he got there his blush was as raw as the sunrise.

'Ye gods . . . is that what he was . . . you mean, there are more of them?'

'Quite a few of them. You really didn't know?'

'I knew he . . . but he was odd that way. Always had been. That was why I wasn't surprised he'd taken Bella's costume . . .'

He was stumbling, finding there was no prompter.

'Not surprised, perhaps, but you were very angry. Was he there waiting for you in the lavatory when you went in?'

He twisted round in his seat so quickly that I was half-way to my feet, ready to throw myself over the door and run.

'How do you know about that?'

'Never mind that. The fact is, you came straight off stage, went into the lavatory and there was Migson waiting for you in Bella's flying costume.'

'Do the police know about this?'

'Yes.'

A lie almost certainly. When I'd last spoken to the inspector he'd said nothing about it and I didn't think Vincent Colvin would have told him. But when you're on a lonely road with a man wanted for murder the occasional lie is only sensible. He groaned and said something I didn't catch. I asked him to repeat it.

'Damn all amateur theatricals.'

He began to talk, slowly at first, then with increasing anger. The root of the trouble had been eight years ago when his college decided to put on *Love's Labours Lost* in its garden at the end of the summer term. I'd been at Oxford instead of Cambridge but I could imagine the kind of thing, Shakespeare mouthed by earnest undergraduates, spectators munched by mosquitoes, fruit cup in the interval. And since no contact with women must be allowed to disturb the virgin bodies or minds of twenty-year-old students, all the women's parts taken by men, as in Shakespeare's time. Which was how Migson came to be Rosaline to Charles Courts' Berowne, starting something that had proved much longer lasting and more irritating than the worst mosquito bite.

'You know the part?'

'The whitely wanton with a velvet brow?'

'Yes. Migson was good, in a creepy sort of way. Too good. Looking back, I can see he felt this tremendous excitement in dressing as a woman, walking like a woman. And as for the love scenes with him . . . well, I suppose it all looked decorous enough . . .'

After all, a fair part of Cambridge would be looking on

through its opera glasses.

'. . . but there was this feeling from him all the time . . .'

His voice trailed away, then he almost shouted:

'I hated it. Hated it. I was glad when the play was over. I told everybody I wouldn't act again until I could do it properly with a woman, and I kept to it.'

'But Migson wouldn't go away?'

'I froze him out. I just made it clear I didn't want anything more to do with him.'

'And he accepted that?'

'I thought he had. It's different at college, I suppose. You have all your friends round you and if you want to keep away from somebody they protect you.'

I could imagine it and felt sorry for Migson. Talented, handsome Charles would be at the centre of a social group that made a hedge as cold and whippy against intruders as the one alongside us.

'Then in London I started to make some kind of name for myself in the theatre and I suppose he heard about it. He wrote me letters suggesting we should meet. He even sent me a cigarette case with a silly inscription. I sent it back, of course.'

'And you wouldn't see him?'

'No. I didn't reply to his letters.'

'Did you know he was working for the Lord Chamberlain's department?'

'No. He'd hardly have admitted that to an actor, and it wasn't what you'd call a distinguished profession, was it?'

Poor Migson.

'So when he turned up at the dress rehearsal that day . . .?'

He faced me, one hand still gripping the steering wheel like a rope in a rough sea.

'That was the most complete surprise to me. I was so angry I thought everybody must have seen it.'

'We thought you were angry about the censorship.'

'I must have acted better than I thought, then. I had no doubt whatsoever that he'd wormed his way in there to get at me.'

'Why didn't you say something?'

'Would you have said something? How could I explain that this creepy little man had some sort of horrible . . . what can I say . . . some sort of obsession with me?'

'Especially with Bella there?'

He turned his profile to me and didn't answer.

'Did you say anything to him after the dress rehearsal?'

He shook his head.

'I took care to keep well away from him. I thought if he could see I wasn't taking any notice of him, he'd go away.'

'But he didn't. He was there in the lavatory next day.'

'Yes. I didn't see him at first. I'd just come off stage and you know what a shouting match that had been, so I was pretty angry in any case. I went into one of the cubicles. He must have been hiding in the other one because . . . oh God . . .'

He shivered and rubbed his gloved hands over his face.

'What happened?'

'His arm . . . came sliding in under the door. I could see from the sleeve that he'd got himself into Bella's costume. Then that awful wheedling voice of his.'

'What was he saying?'

'I don't know. Asking to see me afterwards, I think. Anyway, I stamped on his hand. He let out a howl and I thought that would make him bolt, but he just went back inside the next cubicle and went on talking to me, pleading. I shouted at him to go away. Then luckily somebody came in. I don't know who it was, but he scared Migson away. I stayed in there until this other person had gone, then made a bolt for my dressing room.'

'What happened next time you saw him?'

'The next time I saw him was when they lifted him out of that damned basket, still in Bella's costume. And if you're going to ask me how he got in there I've no more idea than you, probably less.'

'Did you kill him?'

'No. If I'd got my hands on him, I might have. The fact is, I didn't.'

'Why don't you go and tell the police what you've told me?'

The set of his jaw was my only answer. Some women

paid five guineas to see that set jaw from a seat in the front stalls. I was seeing it from a few inches away and didn't feel in the least grateful. Either he'd killed Migson or he was too vain to admit publicly to sitting on a lavatory seat while a man in woman's costume made propositions to him under the door. If I hadn't been annoyed with him, on Migson's behalf, I might have been more sympathetic.

'Well, what do you propose to do about it then? Grow a beard and go to South America?'

'I've told you what I'm going to do. I'm going to see Bella. Will you come with me or won't you?'

I said I wanted to see Bella too and sat there while he went through the laborious process of re-starting the engine.

I'd expected that we'd head for Wantage and the Vale, but he passed the signpost in that direction and kept straight on through the agricultural outskirts of Reading. The road stretched across fields caught in the first hard frost of winter and the only vehicle we passed was a cart loaded with brussels sprouts. A red sun was inching up over the horizon. Charles stared straight ahead, face grim under his motoring cap. I began to wonder where we were going and what his game was. I started calculating my chances if I decided to open the door and jump out. We were doing all of twenty miles an hour, so it would mean a broken arm at best, then a chase over fields with no certainty of winning. I shouted to ask him where we were going, but he pretended not to hear above the noise of the engine.

After two miles or so Charles turned off into a side road that was little more than a farm track and we slowed down. He seemed to know exactly where he was going. If I'd decided to jump out this would have been the time to do it, but in the last half mile the situation had changed. Groping around beside the seat, my fingers had closed on a heavy spanner and I now had it firmly in my grasp. Armed with that, I could afford to give Charles the benefit of the doubt for just a little longer.

The track went on through an open gateway and onto a long stretch of rough grass, more of a common than a field. About half a mile away the ground sloped up to a farmhouse set in a clump of trees. Closer to us was an enormous barn with a sagging roof. It looked half derelict, but there'd been a recent attempt to patch the roof with planks and new tarpaulin. Beside it, obviously newly built, was a wooden tower about fifteen feet high, looking like a modern design for a gibbet. Charles swung the car towards the barn. I noticed a single track in the frosty grass leading in the same direction, too wide for ordinary bicycle wheels. It looked as if somebody had gone to the barn before us that morning on a motorbicycle and hadn't come back. As Charles brought the car to a halt beside the barn and switched off the engine I tightened my grip on the spanner.

He came round to my side and opened the door for me. I kept the spanner in my right hand as I jumped down, hidden in a fold of my skirt. I was careful to let him keep a couple of steps ahead of me as we walked along the side of the barn and round the end. There was a sound of hammering coming from it and somebody was whistling. Do assistant assassins whistle? Come to think of it, I knew of operas where they sing. The barn doorway was wide enough to let in two loaded hay carts side by side, but there was no smell of hay. The smell, as I stood in the weak sunshine and let Charles step inside, was of petrol as in the motor car, and something persistent and sickly sweet that I couldn't identify. From where I was standing it looked dark inside, but I was aware of something in there, something like a brooding giant locust, a thousand times magnified. Whatever I'd expected, this wasn't it.

'Arthur.'

Charles' cry echoed round the barn. The hammering and whistling stopped. He'd disappeared into the half darkness and I followed cautiously, still holding my spanner. After the first few seconds my eyes adjusted and I began to see things – a tool bench, a pile of fuel cans and, rearing over it all, still indistinct in the gloom, the giant locust. I couldn't see Charles now, but I heard his voice as if coming out of the insect.

'Well, Arthur, have you fixed it?'

'Nearly. She'll be ready to go in another five minutes.'

It was a slow Berkshire voice, unreasonably reassuring.

'She'd better be. We want to get off while the weather's clear.'

I put my spanner down on the work bench among a clutter of other tools and walked gingerly over the stone-flagged floor towards the thing. The sickly-sweet smell was coming from its wings – wings out of a legend, easily forty feet across. Charles and a little jockey-like man in a tweed cap were standing beside it, lit by the small flame of an oil lamp.

Charles smiled at me. He seemed already to have taken comfort from being close to the thing.

'Here we are, Miss Bray. Have you ever seen an aeroplane before?'

TWENTY

IT WAS TOWERING OVER US, its double wings a cage of
wires and struts, the smell of petrol stifling. It looked at
the same time monstrous and flimsy.

'What are you proposing to do with it?'

'Fly it to Bella.'

'As simple as that?'

'Penwardine can bolt his gates against me. He can't bolt
the skies.'

'You're not proposing to fly it through his front door?'

'I shan't need to. One of the things about aeroplanes is
that people can't resist coming out to have a look at them.'

'Even supposing Bella comes running out, what
happens then?'

'I talk to her. That's all I'm asking for, a few words with
her.'

'Suppose her husband comes running out too?'

'That's why I need your help. You're used to that sort of
thing. I'm sure you can think of some way of distracting
him while I talk to Bella.'

If Charles thought Suffragette demonstrations were
training for heading off outraged husbands, he might be
in for a disappointment.

'Does this presume I'll be flying with you?'

'Yes. It's all right, Arthur's been up with me three times,
haven't you Arthur?'

'Yes, and down again.'

Charles gave him a look, and he turned away whistling.

'Bella's always begging me to take her up. You know it
would probably make you only the third British woman to
go up in an aeroplane?'

145

And the first, I thought, in an aeroplane flown by a man wanted for murder.

'Of course, if you're nervous . . .'

'I'm not nervous.' Which wasn't entirely true. 'What I'm worrying about is what we do if we get there. Are you proposing to land on his lawn?'

'If it's big and flat enough. If not, there's bound to be a paddock.'

'And then what? Are you thinking of kidnapping Bella?'

I had visions of the thing swooping down and flying away, with Bella hanging from it like a rabbit from a bird of prey.

'I couldn't do that even if I wanted to. Once we've landed outside the house, we shan't be able to take off again.'

I must have looked as puzzled as I felt. Arthur stopped whistling and said, as if it explained everything:

'She's the Wright model, miss. She needs tracks and her launching tower.'

Charles said: 'That's the thing you saw outside. The Wright planes use a track and a kind of catapult to help them get airborne. Without that, we can't take off again.'

I knew, from what he'd said about flying, that this strange assemblage must be important to Charles. Probably expensive too.

'How will you get it back?'

'It has to come on a cart,' Arthur said. He was beginning to look doubtful.

'But suppose Lord Penwardine won't let you take it away?'

Charles said, trying to sound unconcerned: 'Well, in that case I'll have lost my aeroplane, won't I?'

The look of shock, almost of bereavement, on Arthur's face told me this was a possibility they hadn't discussed.

'Mr Courts . . .'

'Not now, Arthur. Well, Miss Bray, are you game to come with me or aren't you?'

The only sensible answer was no.

'Yes,' I said.

I helped them wheel it out. There was a long piece with

smaller wings that stuck out at the front or back – I wasn't
sure which – and they asked me to support that while they
each took one of the big wings and pushed. Somewhere in
the tricky and patient process of getting it out of the barn
and into the sunlight I stopped being 'Miss Bray' to
Charles and became 'Nell'.

'Steady as she goes, Nell. Hold her there a moment.'

Charles seemed happy now he'd got his way, as if he'd
managed to put the murder charge to the back of his
mind. There was no doubting the urgency of his need for
those few words with Bella, but why? A fond farewell
before he gave himself up to the police? An appeal to her
not to tell them something she knew? Or perhaps it was
more complicated. He knew Bella had been away from her
dressing room in that long interval, knew her suspicions
about Migson. Suppose Charles hadn't killed Migson but
believed Bella had? Was Sidney Carton on wings flying to
tell her that she must keep quiet and let him take the
blame?

'Left a bit, Nell. Now hold it there while we turn her
round.'

There was a wooden track on the grass with a metal strip
running along the middle of it, and a small wheel under
the aeroplane had to be slotted into the metal strip. While
we were doing that I put my hand on a wing and it came
away sticky with the cloying, sweet smell I'd noticed.

'Careful, miss,' Arthur said. 'I've been putting some
dope on a patch. It's not quite dry yet.'

'Dope?'

'What we use to stiffen the cotton over the wings.'

'Cotton wings?'

'Yes, just like shirts. And the dope's made from boiled
tapioca.'

So we were taking to the skies on gents' shirting and
nursery pudding. I asked Charles how far away we were
from the Penwardine estate.

'A bit over thirty miles. Don't worry, this model's done
fifty with a passenger.'

I couldn't help remembering that Charles' personal best
was twenty-nine.

There were two seats in the middle of the wings, no more than semi-circles of wood with a metal rail a few inches high behind them. The one on the left, for the pilot, had levers on both sides of it. The passenger seat was next to the engine with the fuel tank just above it. Two long chains, like huge bicycle chains, ran from the engine to twin propellers behind the wings. Behind those was a long, kite-like arrangement that Arthur said was the rudder. There was a nerve-twisting wait while Charles and Arthur hitched a rope from the plane to a heavy weight on the top of the launching tower. Once we were settled, with the engine going, Arthur would let the weight drop and we'd be up and away. The two of them came walking towards me over the grass, the frost on it thawing now the sun was climbing. When Charles wasn't looking, Arthur gave a little pat to the wing, like the Arab saying farewell to his horse. I wished I hadn't seen that.

'Well, are we ready?'

'What about the lady's clothes, Mr Courts?'

Arthur was sent to fetch the goggles from the motor car. I found a piece of oily cotton rag to tie my hat on and, thinking it would be windy in flight, turned my tweed skirt into makeshift breeches by making holes in it with a screwdriver and threading through baler twine. I wished I had Bella's flying outfit of aviation blue leather, until I remembered what happened to the last person who'd borrowed it. I settled on the seat, feet braced against a horizontal strut, right hand grasping a wing strut between me and the engine. After a few words with Arthur, Charles climbed up beside me. He was wearing a leather helmet that buckled under his chin. The engine coughed and throbbed into life.

'All right, Arthur.'

I glanced round. Arthur had taken up position by the wooden tower, ready to release the weight. Charles raised his arm and lowered it, and I took a tighter grip on the strut as we began to move.

People have asked me what it feels like to take off in an aeroplane and I have to tell them that I still don't know. At the time I was conscious of the noise, a rush of air and a

148

kind of buck that was, I suppose, the aeroplane leaving its launching track. I didn't realise we were flying until I saw an oddly shaped shadow keeping pace with us on the grass and realised it was our own and we were in the air above it. By that point we were flying out of the field, clearing a hedge by a foot or two. Charles moved one of the wooden leavers and, as we turned, I could see the barn and the launching tower, with Arthur waving beside it. Our shadow, slick as a weasel, slid across the flat Berkshire fields, fifty feet or so below us now. The huge wings beside us, shirts and tapioca, throbbed with the pulse of the engine. The smaller wings of the front elevator cut the blue sky ahead of us. Wind tore at my makeshift scarf and tried to take my hat away. In spite of everything I felt like shouting with excitement at being there. Beside me, Charles' face was serious.

We climbed steadily. From the occasional farmhouse below us, small as the roofs of Alpine Villages as you come down a mountain, I guessed we might be as high as two hundred feet. Before long the Thames came into view. We followed it as it curved round the Chiltern Hills to our right with the Berkshire Downs further away to the left. Charles said something I couldn't hear above the noise of the engine and nodded up ahead of us. I looked in the same direction and saw a railway viaduct crossing the river. It seemed to be a landmark because we flew up to it then turned left, losing the river and following the railway line westwards. There was a village on our right and I could see people running out, pointing upwards. It seemed at any rate to prove Charles' theory that nobody could resist coming out to see an aeroplane. I looked at my watch and saw we'd been in the air for twenty-five minutes.

The railway line glittered in the sun, the main line to Swindon and Bristol, and as good a waymark as you could wish. We passed close to quite a large town, probably Didcot, then there was flat farmland again, and the Downs beginning to rear up on our left as we entered the Vale of the White Horse. The engine's note was reassuringly steady and our shadow was clearing hedges and ditches below us like a hunt in full cry. I began to agree with Bella that this might be the transport of the future. As the Downs grew higher and closer the white horse itself appeared, cut out of the turf on its long chalk hill. It had been there before the Romans, but this was probably the first time it had been used as a signpost for an aeroplane. Charles glanced at it and turned north, away from our guiding railway line. Almost at once I saw parkland below us enclosed by long red walls. There were gates and a drive sloping up between oak trees, leading to a Queen Anne mansion in red brick and honey-coloured stone. Ockton Hall, the Penwardine's residence. From the air it looked as trim and perfect as a doll's house for the most opulent of nurseries.

We circled over the parkland, losing height. There was a village with a church not far from the gates. Inside the walls paths and carriageways crossed the park, deer paused in their grazing to look up at us, but there was no sign yet of human beings. As we turned I noticed a wooded valley and an odd little stone structure on the lip of it that seemed to have carved leaves growing out of the top. But there wasn't much time to look because we were now down to fifty feet or so and, just as he had followed the railway line to get here, Charles was now following the main drive straight up to the front of the house. It was for all the world as if he intended to fly straight in at the front door.

At the last minute we turned at about the height of the attic windows and flew across the stable yard to the right of the house. At last figures came running out, pale faces looking up. At the back of the house was a terrace with steps leading down to a long lawn. The lawn looked more level than the parkland and might have done as a landing place if there hadn't been a big cedar tree in the middle of it. I glanced at Charles and he was looking worried. He turned the aeroplane and to our right was a small paddock with white rails. It seemed to be the only possible place to land close to the house, and Charles' plan depended on that. He looked at me, shrugged and circled.

We came too fast at the outer rail of the paddock, even I could tell that. Charles pulled his levers, the engine

150

coughed and for a moment we seemed to hang motionless in the air. Then the engine caught again and we climbed, turned and made another approach. It still seemed fast and I braced myself for a hard landing. Then Charles said 'damn' loudly enough to hear over the engine, and we cleared the rail between the paddock and the lawn by no more than a good horse might have done. I could hear shouting. I glanced towards the house and there were people on the terrace. In that awful clarity that comes a few seconds before disaster I could even make out individuals – the sleek head and pale face of Lord Penwardine, his mother beside him, as stiffly upright as a caryatid and there, at the end of the row, the red hair of Bella. She was waving, yelling something, as if that would do any good.

The cedar tree was racing towards us. A second before I thought we must hit it there was a crash that rattled every bone in my body, a sharp pain in my cheek, sounds of tearing and cracking all round us. The smell of torn earth and grass was stronger even than the reek of petrol. Then the engine stopped and in the silence I could hear a bird singing from the cedar tree. Charles and I were still in our seats, tilted sideways, but everything around us was wrecked and misshapen like a trampled matchbox. He said, in a normal tone of voice, that he supposed we should get clear because of the petrol and helped me out from among the broken spars and torn fabric. The aeroplane perched woefully on the ripped grass, leaning on one shattered wing.

'She's here,' I said.

Somebody, Lord Penwardine's mother probably, must have exercised strict discipline over the group on the terrace because they'd stopped shouting and were standing in a frozen row, as if for a photograph, with family in the middle, maids and other staff on the outside. As we walked towards them, Lord Penwardine looked horribly embarrassed and I could understand why. There is etiquette and precedent to rely on if a man happens to be thrown from his horse in your garden. Even, in these fast-moving times, the occasional motor smash in the drive might come within the experience of an English country house of the more raffish kind. But aristocratic calm has had few chances to practise on aeroplanes crashlanding on its lawn. In the case where the pilot is generally believed to be the wife's lover, no chance at all. Another British first.

Bella, not being British so unbothered by the lack of precedent, was the first to move. She came down the steps and ran across the lawn towards us. But she must have caught the warning on my face. I could see, as she couldn't, that the formal reception party was on the move and following her. First the Dowager Lady Dorothea, then Lord Penwardine, then, God help us, the butler. Although they didn't break into a run they covered the ground smartly. Behind them, in more confused order, came sundry housemaids, grooms and outdoor staff. Bella glanced round, saw them and had the wit to put her first question to me.

'Nell, what's happened? Are you hurt?'

But Charles didn't follow her lead. He bounded towards her, would have taken her by the wrist if she hadn't drawn away.

'Bella, what's going on? I must speak to you.'

She hissed at him: 'Not now. Later. I'll meet you in . . .'

From over her shoulder a voice cut in with an edge like steel: 'Good morning. Miss Bray, isn't it? I believe we met at your aunt's house.'

Lady Dorothea already had her lorgnette in hand and was as calm as if we were in her drawing room. She totally ignored Charles and the crippled aeroplane. Behind her Lord Penwardine stood, trying not to look at Bella, two muscular grooms or gardeners like mastiffs at his heels.

'Yes,' I said. 'I'm afraid we've made rather a mess of your lawn.'

Charles had miscalculated. Even if I had been able to distract Lord Penwardine, which had never seemed likely, his mother was a tougher proposition. I glanced at him and he looked furious. Bella had turned away from him. I guessed she'd signalled something and he didn't like it.

'You seem to be injured, Miss Bray. You must come inside and let us attend to it.'

I thought I'd probably gashed my cheek on a broken wing spar, but it didn't feel very serious. On the other hand, entry to the house might give me a chance to speak to Bella and I had my own reasons for wanting to do that, whatever happened to Charles.

Lord Penwardine wasn't managing the trick of ignoring Charles quite as well as his mother. There was a twitch in his shoulder that looked as if it wanted to drive home a punch. Lady Dorothea saw it at a glance and acted.

'George, would you be kind enough to show Miss Bray to my drawing room? Isabella, please find Marie and tell her to bring the first-aid box.'

For a moment I thought it wasn't going to work, as both Lord Penwardine and Bella stayed frozen in their own worlds. Then, with the air of a monolith moving, Lord Penwardine took a few steps towards me.

'If you'd care to come with me, Miss Bray . . .'

I did care. It might perhaps give Charles a few seconds with Bella and he'd paid heavily enough for them. But Penwardine's mother wasn't allowing that.

'Isabella.'

It was like a whip crack. Bella gave a shrug, turned without looking at any of us and ran up the steps and into the house. Lord Penwardine and I followed more sedately. From the terrace I looked back. The outdoor staff had formed a ring round Charles and his aeroplane. A lad had been sent running towards the lodge gates.

'This way.'

Lord Penwardine opened French windows and I stepped through into a room that smelt of wood smoke and looked as if nothing in it had changed since Pitt was Prime Minister. From there you couldn't see Charles or the flying machine at all.

TWENTY-ONE

MARIE MUST HAVE BEEN ALL of eighty, a wrinkled and bad-tempered Breton woman who dragged wooden splinters out of the gash on my cheek with blunt fingers and dabbed iodine relentlessly, making hissing noises through her teeth. I gathered she'd been Lady Dorothea's nursemaid. All the time she sat there on a straight-backed gilt chair watching critically – me, not Marie's nursing technique. We'd moved by then into her own drawing room, an exquisite eighteenth-century affair of dusky pinks and ivories, all faded, with a silver fan in the grate instead of a fire. It made me conscious of my mistreated tweed skirt and my heavy boots, the oily scarf and goggles lying on the chair beside me. She talked about my aunt, about the weather, my opinion of Paris in the winter, and I did my best to keep up the tone.

All the time I was thinking how much I disliked Lord Penwardine. Charles' flight here, a failure in other respects, had at least shifted the focus for me. In the two days since the murder, circumstances had kept me looking at the London end of it. That group on the terrace had been a powerful reminder that three of the people involved – Bella, Lord Penwardine and Piggy Ditchbrake – had shifted rapidly to the sanctuary of Ockton Hall. Although Piggy had not been on view so far, I was convinced he wouldn't be far away and there were questions I wanted to put to him as well as Bella.

At long last Marie gathered up her lint and plaster and withdrew, leaving my cheek feeling worse than when she'd started.

'You'll stay to lunch with us, Miss Bray?'

I said yes, thank you. I sensed that business was about to begin from the way she sat up even more straightly. As she moved, she couldn't avoid a little grimace of pain. I remembered she'd had a bad back on the journey down. A lesser woman would have taken to a chaise longue.

'The person who was driving your flying machine, do I take it that he's the actor?'

Her voice pitched it somewhere between pickpocket and polecat.

'Charles Courts, yes. It's his own aeroplane.'

'What was his purpose in bringing it here?'

'He wanted to speak to your daughter-in-law.'

A long sigh. She stared out at the bare wisteria branches round the window. When she spoke again her voice was low and confiding, but it had a curious impersonal quality about it, as if making a public speech to an audience of one.

'You know, Miss Bray, I was very pleased when George told me he intended to marry Isabella. Does that surprise you?'

'Why should it?'

That wasn't the right reaction but she pressed on.

'I know some people believed that, coming from a family as old as ours, he should have chosen a British girl. I've never been of that narrow way of thinking. We should always be ready to welcome new blood of the right kind.'

I just stopped myself saying Count Dracula would agree with her.

'Perhaps Isabella didn't have all the polish one might expect in a girl brought up here, but I recognised she had qualities of her own and I was ready to welcome them.'

Like two million dollars. But I didn't interrupt. The woman was so convinced of the divine right of the Penwardines that it would be like breaking my fingernails on granite. The voice dropped.

'And I hoped – I know George and I both hoped – that there would be an heir. I've noticed in other marriages of the kind that American girls do seem to be good at producing sons.'

'How very fortunate. Do you suppose it's something

155

they put in their feed?'

She ignored me, still in confiding mode.

'Unfortunately, this didn't happen with Isabella. George and I were very disappointed, of course, but we never reproached her with it, never.'

I bit my tongue.

'That's why her ingratitude hurt George so much. He's given Isabella more freedom than most men in his position would have contemplated. And she abused it, Miss Bray. She abused it most cruelly.'

I might be a guest under her roof, but there were limits.

'Was that why he encouraged Piggy Ditchbrake and his friends to break up her performance?'

She absorbed my ill manners, closing her eyes and taking a deep breath.

'George had nothing to do with that. It's hardly surprising that his friends should resent what she was doing on his behalf. George has very loyal friends. But he had nothing to do with it himself.'

'Really? He wasn't far away from the theatre earlier in the evening.'

She smiled. I didn't expect that.

'Miss Bray, I really am most relieved to hear you say that. It's a weight off my mind.'

'Why?'

'The day after that . . . unfortunate occurrence at the theatre, a man from Scotland Yard called on us. He questioned my son most impertinently on where he'd been the evening before. At the time neither George nor I could understand it. Now of course I see why. It was because of your mistake.'

'You think I was mistaken?'

'Oh, I'm sure you meant no harm. But of course you'd only met George once in your life. It would be easy to be mistaken and of course the police would be duty bound to investigate. Please understand, Miss Bray, that I don't blame you, not in the least.'

'And the police were satisfied?'

'Of course. As it happened, George had been at home with me all evening. The man from Scotland Yard was very apologetic about it in the end.'

'I'm sure he was.'

I could see now why I'd been separated from Charles, welcomed through gritted teeth as a guest. It was to hammer home this idea that I couldn't have seen Lord Penwardine near the Crispin. But I had seen him and a regiment of dowager ladies couldn't convince me otherwise.

A gong sounded, a low, respectful boom.

'Luncheon. It's an informal meal when there's just the family. I hope you'll make allowances for us.'

It was as informal as a court martial. There were the four of us, Lord Penwardine, his mother, Bella and myself, at the end of an oak table big enough for a dozen. Plates of cold beef, mutton and winter salad were laid out on a long sideboard, festive as funeral wreaths, and two servants attended to our needs, speaking in respectful whispers. Lord Penwardine, the last to come in, nodded a greeting at his mother and me, totally ignored Bella and accepted cold beef with the air of a man taking on yet another duty. If he was pleased that his wandering wife had come back, he gave no sign of it. His mother talked about the pictures in the Uffizi, pausing now and again, with her head on one side, for my valuable opinion. Bella sat opposite me, toying with winter salad, but for all the chance I had of speaking to her about anything that mattered she might as well have been ten miles away.

Now and again she'd look at me and I knew she was desperate to ask what had happened to Charles. The windows of the dining room gave no view of the back lawn and there was nothing to suggest that the estate had recently been invaded by an aeroplane. Outside the park sloped to the main gate, half a mile away. To the left it dipped more steeply to the wooded valley. On the lip of the valley there was a huge pineapple in honey-coloured sandstone, the kind of thing beloved of eighteenth-century folly builders. I remarked on it, as a change from Florentine art, not mentioning that I'd noticed it from the air.

Bella said: 'It's a summer house.'

Before Lady Penwardine could get back to pictures I

said, directing the question mainly at Lord Penwardine:

'Did Mr Ditchbrake get home safely?'

They froze, all three of them.

'He must have had an uncomfortable night, being questioned by the police. It was kind of Lord Penwardine to let him take the carriage to Paddington.'

Lord Penwardine had stopped eating. Both Bella and his mother were looking at him.

'Mr Ditchbrake has a house in the village.'

He nodded down the drive and towards the gates. It was hardly an answer.

'Has he? Perhaps I'll call on him on my way out.'

Lady Dorothea said: 'You're acquainted with Mr Ditchbrake?'

'Slightly. I should like to know him better.'

Bella said suddenly: 'You won't find him at home.'

Both mother and son swivelled towards her. Neither looked pleased.

'I tried to call on him yesterday, Nell. His groom told me he hadn't been home for a week.'

Yet he'd taken Lord Penwardine's carriage to Paddington, a stage on his journey back to Berkshire.

Bella said, her eyes on her husband's face: 'His sister might know. I saw her walking in the park this morning.'

There was a challenge in the way she said it, and I could tell the words had a significance I didn't understand. Still, I was surprised by Lord Penwardine's reaction. He dropped his fork and, as he stared at Bella, his face went red, slowly and painfully. Then he looked away and snapped at the servant who'd leapt forward with another fork. Lady Dorothea said to the other servant, in a voice that would have sent cabinet ministers scurrying:

'I'm sure Miss Bray would like some trifle.'

It cloyed the mouth like unwanted charity. When we'd all made a token attempt at eating some, Lady Penwardine signalled to the servants and took her stand at the sideboard alongside the half-empty plates and dishes. Two large metal containers were brought and like a woman performing a ritual she scraped the contents of the dishes into them. They went in hugger-mugger, cold meats and

158

salad along with the trifle. Bella watched but said nothing.
Lady Dorothea turned towards me, wiping her hands on a linen napkin.

'As you see, Miss Bray, I can't abide waste. Our old people are grateful for what we leave.'

I thanked her for her hospitality and asked for directions to the nearest railway station.

'Thomas will drive you there in the pony cart. I'm sure you won't mind if he delivers the lunch to our old people first.'

Nicely done, I thought. In uninvited by aeroplane, out with the kitchen scraps in a pony cart. As we all walked out to the hall I wondered if she'd try to keep me under guard. I'm sure she wanted to, but her resources were overstretched because Lord Penwardine mumbled something about wanting a word with her. He clearly hadn't recovered from what Bella had said at the lunch table. His mother gave him a glance and diagnosed trouble.

'Your study, shall we?'

He opened a door on the other side of the hall.

Bella said loudly: 'I'll see Nell to the pony cart.'

She led the way at a walk so fast it was almost a run, through a succession of doors to an open corridor along one side of the stable yard. The servants followed with the food containers. A governess cart with a tubby grey pony was drawn up ready. Bella glanced at the servants and drew me over to the far side of the yard.

'Nell, I must see Charles. Tell him I'll be at the lodge by the west gate. I'll wait there till he comes.'

'It might not be easy. The last I saw he'd been pretty well put under guard.'

'Who by?'

'The servants. But I'm afraid it's worse than that.'

'How?'

She was dead white. Even her lips had hardly any colour in them. There was no way of breaking it gently.

'There's a warrant out for his arrest, for murdering Migson.'

She gave a little cry, then checked it when one of the servants glanced in our direction.

'He didn't, Nell.'
'How do you know that?'
'Because my husband did.'
'Can you prove that?'
'Yes.'
'Really prove? Prove in a court of law?'
She bit her lip.
'Not yet. Not quite yet. That's why I came back here, to this prison of a place, because I'm going to prove it. I'm not leaving here until I have proof that will convince anybody, whatever strings those two try to pull. But Charles doesn't know that. I haven't had a chance to tell him. And if they arrest him now . . . Oh Nell, you must get him to me.'

The food containers had been lifted into the governess cart. The groom was waiting at the pony's head, talking to one of the indoor servants who was holding my coat, goggles and battered hat.

'Bella, if you know anything about this murder you must tell somebody. Tell the police. Tell me, if you like.'

She stared down at the cobblestones.

'I suppose I should. But not the police. The police will believe him and his mother, like they did when they said he was at home in Park Lane all evening.'

'And he wasn't?'

'Of course he wasn't, Nell. He was there, at the theatre.'

'Actually inside the theatre?'

'Just outside it.'

'When?'

'After all the trouble. When we had to hold up the play. When that man was murdered.'

'How do you know?'

She looked me full in the face and said, slowly and distinctly: 'I know my husband was there because I saw him.'

'Tell me. Tell me from the time you came off stage.'

She took a deep breath.

'I went to the dressing room and put my coat on over my costume. I thought the play was over, ruined. I didn't think we'd be starting again. I knew it was his fault and guessed he'd be out there somewhere. I went rushing out of the stage door to tell him what I thought of him.'

'How long did this take after you came off stage?'

'I didn't waste time. I was too angry. Perhaps five minutes.'

'And you found him?'

'Oh yes. I found him.'

'Where?'

'You remember there's a public house just across the street? Guggles was on his own at an upstairs window, watching people being thrown out of the theatre. I wanted to go up to him there and then, but I thought I'd wait and see what he did next. I stood back in a doorway so he couldn't see me. Then after a while Piggy Ditchbrake came running down the street, looking as if he'd been in a fight, and Guggles came down to talk to him.'

'Did Piggy see you?'

'No. Guggles said something to Piggy, then Piggy went rushing off towards the stage door. So then I jumped out at Guggles and held him by the coat so that he couldn't get away. I thought he was going to die of mortification. He doesn't mind murdering his wife, but he can't have a row with her in a public street.'

'How long did this go on?'

'Some time. I was telling him what I thought of him for breaking up the play and people were pushing and rushing all round us, nobody taking any notice. I suppose they thought it was all part of the riot. Then somebody, I don't know who, shouted out that they were going to start the play again. I let go of Guggles and bolted back inside to get changed.'

'So you didn't leave him until the play was about to start again?'

'No. I hardly had time to get changed. You saw me.'

'Why didn't you tell me this at the time?'

'I thought you'd be mad with me for leaving the theatre.'

'And you think this proves your husband killed Migson?'

'Yes. Piggy was the one who did the dirty work, but it was Guggles who planned it. And it worked, except that wretched little man was mincing around in my costume, so they shot him instead. Guggles must have got the shock of his life when I jumped out at him. Anyway, all I have to do now is find out where he's hiding Piggy. Piggy's pathetic. He'll confess.'

The colour was coming back into her face. There was something I had to explain to her but she wouldn't like it and there were questions to be settled first.

'You think Piggy Ditchbrake is somewhere on the estate?'

'Of course he is.'

'You're probably right about that. I noticed your husband was shaken when you talked about seeing his sister here.'

Bella looked ill at ease.

'There might be another reason for that.'

'What?'

'Oh, I might as well tell you. I shouldn't have raised it in the first place. After all, it's not poor Louise's fault.'

'Louise being Piggy's sister?'

'That's right. She's the woman I told you about. You know, the childhood sweetheart. The one Guggles was going to marry before his mother made him marry me for my damned dollars. They've been having an affair ever since we got back from honeymoon. Guggles knows I know, but we don't talk about it.'

Any other time I might have been sorry for both of them, but there was worse news for Bella than that.

'What you've just told me doesn't prove your husband or Piggy Ditchbrake killed Migson.'

'But they were there. I saw them.'

'They may have been outside the theatre, but on your evidence your husband couldn't have been backstage when the shot was fired. First he was at the window of a public house, then he was down in the street with you telling him what you thought of him. I'm sorry, but you've just provided him with an alibi.'

'But Piggy . . . Piggy was the one who actually fired the shot.'

I shook my head. We hadn't had a chance to speak since the murder. She wasn't to know that my hand on his arm

162

at the time when the shot was fired gave Piggy his own alibi. As I explained she kept shaking her head but I could see from her expression that she understood what I was saying.

'But they must have done it, Nell. Why did Piggy dash off like that? Why are they keeping him hidden away?'

'I don't know.'

And yet I was beginning to have the glimmerings of an idea, not one I could discuss with Bella.

'Nell, what can we do? You can't let them arrest Charles.'

'I've no choice.'

'Tell them . . . tell them what you like. Tell them I shot him.'

'But you were outside, keeping watch on your husband.'

'Oh.'

She thumped her fist against her thigh, screwed up her eyes in frustration.

'I must speak to Charles. You'll get him there, won't you? The west gate lodge.'

I said I would if I could. We walked together across the courtyard.

'You'd better go off in the pony cart in case she's watching. When you get outside the yard you can say you've forgotten something, hop off and go and find Charles.'

She stood watching as we drove out of the yard. As soon as we were on the gravel drive to the side of it I called to the groom that I'd forgotten something and not to wait for me, opened the door at the back and stepped down. A kitchen courtyard, piled with crates and boxes, led to a path that took me eventually to the terrace at the back of the house. On the lawn Charles was standing beside the crumpled aeroplane, smoking a cigarette. Two of the outdoor staff, also smoking, were standing in a relaxed way and talking to him, but he had the air of a man under guard. I was going over to him, thinking of a way to distract the guards and deliver Bella's message, when two men appeared from the other side of the lawn. They wore blue uniforms and were walking fast and purposefully. Charles threw his cigarette away. The garden workers drew back, leaving him on his own.

I was a few yards away when the first policeman reached

163

Charles. He was a country officer and clearly not used to this, red-faced and ill at ease. Still, he'd mastered his lines.

'Are you Mr Charles Courts, sir?'

Charles nodded.

'Then we must ask you to come with us, sir.'

'Why?'

'There's a warrant out for your arrest, sir. On a charge of murdering Mr Matthew Migson.'

Charles saw me, thought of saying something then decided against it. He turned to the garden workers and nodded at the aeroplane.

'Could you rig a tarpaulin or something over that? A man named Arthur will come and collect it.'

They nodded. Without another word Charles went with the policemen across the lawn. They probably had a vehicle parked on the drive. No question of letting him set foot in Lord Penwardine's house. I noticed he'd left his flying helmet and goggles on the grass, picked them up and put them on the aviator's seat.

One of the men said: 'Don't worry, miss, we'll look after it for him.'

'Doesn't look as if he'll be wanting them for a while,' the other one said.

TWENTY-TWO

I WENT SLOWLY BACK TO the stable yard and waited till the groom returned in the governess cart with the empty food tins.

'Ready to go now, miss?'

I said yes, I was ready. The Dowager Lady Penwardine had more or less ordered me off the premises and might cross-question the groom to make sure I'd gone. We trotted up the road to the gates, ten feet of heraldic wrought iron, firmly shut. I found a pencil and notebook in my pocket and scribbled a few words, steadying it on my lap against the jolting of the cart. 'Sorry, message undelivered. Gone.' It wasn't much for Bella, waiting over at the west lodge, but for her own sake I couldn't risk more, in case it fell into unfriendly hands. If the Penwardines employed a gate-keeper the governess cart must be beneath his notice, because the groom had to get down to open a wing of the wrought iron himself.

While he was doing it I said: 'I don't want to go to the station quite yet. Would you drop me off at the village?'

'It's not much of a village, miss.'

'I'd like a look at the church while I'm here.'

He was glad enough to let me down at the church gate instead of the longer jog to the station. As I got out I gave him half a crown and my note.

'The young Lady Penwardine is at the west lodge. Could you go back that way and give this to her, please?'

He touched his cap with his whip and I watched the governess cart roll away down the road. It didn't roll more than two hundred yards or so before coming to rest outside the pub and the groom knotted the reins, jumped

165

down and went inside. All for the best. It meant Bella would have to wait for her message, but the groom was hardly likely to tell Lady Penwardine how he'd spent his time instead of taking me to the station.

The red brick wall round Lord Penwardine's park was the most obvious feature of the landscape. I turned away from the church and followed the road that ran parallel to it until I was round a bend and out of sight from church or pub. Then I threw my hat over the wall, hitched up my skirt and took a running jump at it. It took three tries and a fair part of the skin off my wrists but I managed to get on top of it in the end. I scrambled down, picked up my hat from a bramble bush and tried to get my bearings. I was too far away from the house to be seen without binoculars and there were saplings and brambles growing close to the wall that would give some sort of cover. About a quarter of a mile away to my left was the main drive. To my right the ground sloped away more steeply, meadowland dotted with a few massive oak trees. The wooded valley and the pineapple-shaped summer house must be in that direction.

I kept close to the wall, using the saplings as cover. At one point I startled a great red stag. He stared at me, made a snorting noise, then wheeled and galloped off. His does fell in line obediently behind him and they streamed in a line across the faded grassland, the sun already low and red behind them. As the sun dropped the frost was beginning to settle again. Only three o'clock but it would be dark in an hour or less. I walked on and came to the point where the wall slanted down at the edge of a little valley. The trees in it were as thick as moss and would have given good cover, but I hadn't time to scramble through them. I walked along the edge of the valley, keeping it to my right, until the spiky top of the stone pineapple appeared on my left.

For some reason I still had a vivid picture in my mind of the way it had looked from forty feet or so up in the air – the pineapple itself casting a shadow over the grass, the cleft of the valley behind it and, leading to it from the direction of the house, a trail of footprints. If you walk on grass when it's frosty, it bruises. Later, when the frost melts, that bruise is left as a darker area. From the ground I might not have noticed, but it had been very clear from the aeroplane. That morning, while the frost was still on the grass, somebody had taken the trouble to walk all the way to the pineapple summer house. There might be a dozen reasons for it. I was taking a guess about one of them.

Keeping the pineapple between myself and the house I moved closer to it. The eighteenth-century folly builders had done their work thoroughly, chiselling the curving stone wall into rough squares like the rind of the fruit. Two feet above ground level the curves smoothed themselves out into a stone pediment. I walked round and came to a normal-shaped door, deeply recessed into the stone. When I saw it my heart jumped because the grass in front of it was bruised and trampled by more than one pair of feet, or the same feet several times over. There was no lock on the door, just a wrought-iron ring. I twisted it and pushed and the door swung open.

A voice from inside, a plump, querulous voice, said: 'Is that you at last, Guggles?'

The voice of Piggy Ditchbrake.

I pushed the door wide open and stepped in. Empty bottles fell and rolled over a stone floor. The air seemed even colder than outside, but the smell was of a morning after a party, wine, cigar fumes and weariness. Some light came in through a single window opposite me, more from a pair of candles. They stood on a table in a holder encrusted with their own wax, illuminating an island in the centre of the room that looked as if an untidy slice of gentleman's club had been lifted from Pall Mall and transported there. A wooden lounging chair, plumped out with cushions, stood next to a couch with a disorder of blankets on it. Besides the candlestick the table was cluttered with the remains of cold meat, a copy of *Jorrocks's Jaunts and Jollities*, several used wine glasses, a brandy bottle and an open box of Cuban cigars. In the chair Piggy Ditchbrake lounged, lagged against the cold in overcoat, gloves and balaclava, a glass of brandy in his hand. He was

trying to get me into focus. Two cases of wine and another
brandy bottle were lined up under the window.
'Hello. Thought you were Guggles. Seen you some-
where before, haven't I?'
'Yes.'
I closed the door and crossed towards the window.
''Scuse me not getting up. Seem to have done something
to my fetlock in the rush.'
'What rush?'
'Rush getting down here from town.'
He sounded resentful but not at my presence. He still
seemed to think I'd been sent by Lord Penwardine.
'How much longer have I got to stay here?'
'Don't you remember what Guggles told you?'
It was a safe bet, I thought. He took a gulp of brandy,
looked at me and blinked.
'Till the police stop being interested. Talked to me
already. Kept me in prison all night.'
'Yes, but that was in London. Did you know the police
have been down here today?'
His slack body jerked with alarm, sending the brandy
sloshing round in its glass.
'Here? Looking for me?'
'You don't want to speak to them again, do you? Next
time they might ask you questions you couldn't answer.'
That must have been what worried Lord Penwardine.
Since Piggy had an alibi, he could pay a good lawyer to
have him released on the morning after the murder. Once
out, it had been a reflex of panic to get him out of London
and hide him away. Goodness knows how long he
expected to keep him in the pineapple. The two cases of
wine suggested a long time, but perhaps not so long, given
Piggy's rate of consumption. The mention of the police
had worried him. He downed the brandy in the glass,
poured more.
'Lord Penwardine told you to stay here?'
'Guggles. That's right. Said the police keep on at people.
Bastards just keep on and on and on . . .'
'Why would they do that?'
He glared.

168

'Because some silly little runt bloody well got himself killed when he damned well shouldn't have. 'Scuse my language. You hunt?'

'And you were there.'

'I didn't kill the little runt.'

'But you know who did.'

I was rushing my fences. His eyes came briefly into focus and an attempt at a shrewd look wavered over his face.

'You from the police?'

'No.'

''Spose not. Don't have ladies in the police. What you doing here then?'

Now I'd triggered his suspicion I might as well admit it and see how he reacted.

'I'm a friend of Bella's.'

'Oh. Oh, like that, is it? Thought I'd seen you before.'

'I was there that night at the theatre.'

'I told her what I thought of her. She was up there on the stage and I told her what I thought of her, making her husband look ridilicous . . . rishicul . . .'

He gave up and closed his eyes.

'I helped throw you out, remember?'

His eyes opened.

'Were you the bastard took my horn, 'scuse my language?'

'No, that was somebody else.'

'You tell him I want my horn back. Not fair, taking a man's horn.'

I said I'd mention it. He was frowning now, trying hard to make sense of things, but his problem was that the harder he tried the more quickly he drank. The brandy bottle on the table was nearly empty now. I wondered whether Lord Penwardine's intention was simply that he should drink himself to death, here in the cold summer house. More probably it was just his way of keeping Piggy quiet and obedient. After a few minutes of frowning and muttering to himself he gave up the struggle. His eyes closed again, his mouth fell open and his ripe snores echoed round the dome of the pineapple. For the second time in two days I found myself keeping watch over an unconscious man. I might as well have got married or taken up nursing after all.

He slid down in the chair so that his arms hung limply, almost touching the floor. After contemplating the picture for a while I felt in my pocket and found the twine that I'd used to tie up my skirt for the aeroplane flight. I made a little loop of one end of it, walked quietly over to Piggy and slipped it round his right thumb. He stirred slightly, but didn't wake and snored on while I threaded it round the back of the chair. It was a longer and more involved process to get a loop round his left wrist and knot it firmly, but I managed it. It was the kind of trick my cousins and myself used to play on each other as children and I was glad I hadn't lost the skill. It wouldn't hurt Piggy in the least, as long as he didn't try to get up. A sober man would have been out of it in minutes, but Piggy wouldn't even remember the last time he'd been sober.

After that I removed the brandy bottle and glass from the table, carried them across to the window sill and lined up several more bottles beside them. The window looked out over the valley. There was a clearing in the trees below, with an eighteenth-century architect's idea of a ruined Greek temple. At one time it had probably been connected by a path to the pineapple, an afternoon's stroll for curious ladies and gentlemen. The window catch was stiff. The noise of it opening and the blast of even colder air from outside woke Piggy.

'What's happening? Police, is it the police?'

His head had jerked up, but he hadn't tried to move his arms.

'We were talking about what happened the night at the theatre. Do you remember being thrown out?'

He nodded. It was beginning to creep into his mind that something was wrong, but he still didn't know where.

'But you went in again, didn't you? You went in by the stage door.'

'They didn't stop the earth. Should always remember to stop the earth.'

He said it with some triumph, then a look of pure sadness came over his face.

170

'Missing the hunting season. He can't expect me to stay here for the whole hunting season.'

'Yes, Guggles does expect a lot from his friends, doesn't he? What was that he said to you before you went in at the stage door?'

Piggy snapped his jaws together in what was meant to be a firm line but he must have jarred a bad tooth because he ouched and tried to put out a hand for the brandy glass. It slowly dawned on him what was wrong.

'Tied up. The bastards have tied me up.'

He looked down at his arms and up at me, such puzzlement on his face that I had to think hard about poor Migson to stop myself feeling sorry for him.

'Did you tie me up?'

'Yes. I'll untie you when you tell me why you went back into the theatre.'

He set his jaw, more cautiously this time.

'It's one-way loyalty with the likes of Lord Penwardine, you know. He won't try to protect you when the police find out you lied to them. It will be prison for you. No hunting there and no drink either.'

'Guggles wouldn't do that.' But he sounded uncertain. 'Let me have a drink. Just a little sip of brandy.'

I picked up the brandy bottle from the row on the window sill and flung it out to the frosty air. There was a sound of breaking glass as it hit the Greek temple below. Piggy howled so loudly I was afraid they'd hear him in the house half a mile away.

'Did Guggles tell you to go back in?'

No answer. A bottle of Margaux followed the brandy through the window. I'd had time to read the label, so it made me feel almost as bad as tying up Piggy.

'If you don't tell me, they're all going out and you'll be left here with nothing to drink.'

A second wine bottle made an arc against the white sky and the red setting sun.

'Are you from the Salvation Army?'

The horror in his voice was much greater than when he'd just thought I was from the police. A third bottle went the way of the others. Mist was beginning to rise from the

171

wood and wine fumes mingled with it like the smoke of a sacrifice to connoisseur gods. Piggy writhed and moaned and cursed. I lined up another three bottles on the sill and repeated the question. This time he gave a slow, reluctant nod.

'Why did he tell you to go back?'

I pushed a bottle to the outside of the window ledge. Piggy's eyes hung on it.

'Give me a drink. Just one drink.'

'As soon as you tell me. Were you looking for somebody? Or something?'

It was in my mind that Penwardine and Piggy between them might have rigged up some mechanical device, intended to scare, even kill Bella when she stepped into the basket, and got Migson instead. In that case, Piggy would have to go in to clear away the evidence of it. By the time we got well down the second case, I was sure, his nerve would break and he'd tell me. By that time, the gods of the temple would be as drunk as Piggy himself.

But we never got that far and a case and three-quarters of good Margaux were saved, whatever else was lost, when the door to the pineapple opened and a voice called, tentative at first: 'Piggy.'

Then, alarmed and sharp: 'Piggy, what's happening?'

Piggy's eyes flew wide open. He gasped with relief like a child who's found its nurse.

'Louise. Stop her, Louise. She's mad. She's throwing good drink away.'

Because it was almost dark in the pineapple, outside the small island of guttering candlelight, I couldn't see her face at first, though I knew from the name that she must be Piggy's sister, Penwardine's childhood sweetheart, the woman Bella blamed herself for wronging with her 'damned dollars'. The line of her coat and hat had something familiar about them, but then a lot of women wear fur hats. It wasn't until she stepped forward into the candlelight and I moved from the window that we recognised each other. There was the fair hair escaping from under the hat, the hungry little mouth like a finch's beak.

'Well,' I said, 'I do believe it's Penelope.'

172

TWENTY-THREE

WE STARED AT EACH OTHER. She took a few steps towards me. Piggy went on making small sounds of protest, but she took no notice of him.

'I owe you an apology,' I said.

I'd taken her for a stupid woman. Whatever she was, she wasn't that.

'The first time we met, at the theatre, I really thought you were infatuated with Charles Courts. But that wasn't why you wanted his address, was it? You wanted to spy on him at his home, to find evidence of adultery with Bella so that Lord Penwardine could divorce her and marry you.'

She moved towards Piggy. Her eyes must have been as sharp as her mouth because, even in the dim light, she'd taken in the situation at first glance and seen he was tied to the chair. She undid the twine without comment or surprise, like the latest in the long line of things that a clever little sister does for a not very clever big brother.

'And you were the mystery woman in the Mews, the one Piggy picked up in Lord Penwardine's carriage on the morning after the murder.'

Piggy said weakly: 'Don't talk to her, Lou.'

He got up, managed at second attempt to pick up a corkscrew from the table and lurched across the room to a bottle on the window ledge. When he got it he hugged it against his chest.

'But you didn't catch the train with him, because by then he'd told you the one thing that could throw you off course. He'd told you that Bella had gone back to her husband.'

I sat down in Piggy's chair so that I could look up at her

face. It gave away very little.

'You wanted to know if that was true. And it was true. That was when you stopped pretending. You decided to follow me home because you thought I knew what was happening. You wanted me to persuade Bella to let Lord Penwardine go. Because, as you told me, you were the one who really loved him. Because you wanted to have his baby.'

'I wanted to have his son.'

The correction came so quietly from her half-open lips that I scarcely heard it. Piggy, who'd got the bottle open by now, made a reproachful noise, either at me or his sister.

'But by then I'd got it in my mind that it was Charles Courts you wanted. I thought you were asking me to persuade Bella to leave Charles to you.'

She said nothing. She didn't need to say anything. That flat declaration of the need to have Lord Penwardine's son hung over the room, more chilling than the cold air, more pervasive than the wine fumes.

'You must have been desperate by the time you came to me. You'd been clever and resourceful, you'd put your reputation at risk. Then, just when you were within arm's reach of getting what you'd both wanted for a long time, you heard Bella had gone back to him. After all you'd done and risked.'

She moved across to the open window and closed it tidily. Piggy lodged himself against the sill, eyes swivelling from his sister to me and back again.

'Well, what are you going to do now?'

Her voice was calm and emotionless but her slight lisp gave it a childish quality. I tried to imagine her as a girl of fifteen or so, worshipping the young son and heir, home for the holidays, the two of them riding through the park together. But I could only see them as younger versions of what they were now, the stiff and mother-dominated boy, the girl with the soft blonde hair and sharp little mouth.

'I don't know what I'm going to do.'

It was the truth. I was still trying to come to terms with what I'd found out in the last few minutes. There were no more questions I needed to ask Louise Ditchbrake, and the one answer I needed from her brother I shouldn't get now. I walked to the door, opened it. When I looked back brother and sister were still by the window, he looking up at her, befuddled, she watching me gravely.

It was already dark outside, apart from a few lights in the downstairs rooms of the big house. I wondered if Bella had got my note. Charles would probably be on his way back to London in police custody. I'd told Louise Ditchbrake that I didn't know what I was going to do, but when I thought about it I had no choice. I knew now that Charles had not killed Migson. The question was how to prove that in a way that would satisfy the police. I left Lord Penwardine's estate the way I'd come, across the rough grass of the parkland and over the wall. It was harder this time because I was tired and burdened with a knowledge that I wasn't carrying when I went in. I landed heavily on the road, brushed myself down and walked the short distance to the public house near Lord Penwardine's gates.

At just after five o'clock in the afternoon the place had no customers and the landlord was obliging, though he looked askance at my patched face and battered clothes. He said he'd harness up their pony and trap and take me to the station. The next train wasn't until seven, so there'd be plenty of time. While the lad was catching the pony I sipped sherry and talked to the landlord. He assumed that I'd had business at the big house because that was the only reason a stranger would come to this part of the world. He was proud of the Penwardine family and happy to talk about them, their hunts, their dinner parties and balls, the visits of royalty for shooting. The wall of the bar was respectfully hung with photographs of Penwardine occasions.

I took an interest in a recent one, taken at the hunt ball of the previous season. Lord Penwardine was there in the centre of the picture, Bella next to him, beautifully dressed but uneasy. And there, at the end of the row, looking straight out at the camera, the woman Lord Penwardine had always loved more than his wife.

'I wonder if I might borrow this for a few days? There's a man I recognise in the back row there. I know he'd be interested to see it.'

175

A necessary lie. The landlord was very obliging about it, wrapped up the photograph and handed it to me as I got into the trap. Three hours later I was back in London, unwrapping it in the glass-fronted booth occupied by the stage door-keeper at the Crispin Theatre.

He wasn't best pleased to see me. I belonged, with the *Cinderella* cast, to a bad time and he was now settling down to a long honeymoon with *Minnesota Minny*. Still, he owed me a favour for not telling Shaw or Freeson about his money-raising activities among the devotees of Charles Courts. He looked long and hard at the face I pointed out in the picture.

'She wasn't dressed like that when I saw her.'

'No, of course she wasn't. But is it the same woman?'

Still staring, he wiped the back of his hand across his mouth.

'Yes, it's her all right.'

'You'd swear to that?'

'I hope I don't have to. But yes, if I had to, I'd swear to it.'

I went from the theatre to track down Bernard Shaw and found him eventually as he left a meeting on law reform in Tavistock Street. I walked with him to his home in Adelphi Terrace and, for once, did most of the talking while he had to listen. He'd got me into this, so he could share some of the responsibility. Around midnight we wrote the telegram that went in my name to Bella at her husband's house:

Arriving tomorrow 11 am. Please arrange all characters on stage, including Ditchbrakes. Piggy in pineapple.

Lord Penwardine or his mother would probably read it first, but that didn't matter.

Then home, and not much sleep, only the memory of a pair of determined eyes looking into mine as they must have looked, in the dim light, at the back of an aviation blue flying outfit that should have had Bella inside it. I didn't like the mind behind those eyes, but conceded it a kind of respect.

TWENTY-FOUR

I WENT DOWN ALONE BY as early a train as I could get on a Sunday morning. I'd sent a telegraph the night before to the landlord of the public house alongside the Penwardine estate asking him to send his pony and trap to meet me at the railway station. It was there waiting for me, the pony fidgeting in the winter sunshine. As we came up the village street I saw a confusion of gigs and motor cars, half a dozen or so, sorting themselves out near the gateway of the church. A smart gig drawn by an iron-grey hackney was the first away, going towards the park gates. The boy from the pub had drawn up his pony respectfully to wait for the church crowd to disperse and I asked him whose the gig was.

'That's Lady Dorothea's.'

There'd been a man beside her driving the gig, but I had no chance to see if he was Lord Penwardine. I told the boy I'd walk the rest of the way, got down and paid him.

The main gateway was open. I walked down the long drive, through the park with its grazing deer to the great house of rose brick and honey-coloured stone. They were fine things and the Penwardines, so the pub landlord had told me, had lived there for two hundred years. And yet, I thought, if the Penwardines had no heir, house and park wouldn't fly away at the stamp of a fairy godmother's foot. The deer would still breed, the sun still warm the stonework. And yet a part of me wanted to walk away and leave it all just as it was.

I went up a flight of steps to the great front door. It was opened as soon as I knocked, so the butler must have been waiting. I gave him my name.

'Lady Penwardine is expecting you. She's waiting for you in the library.'

But Bella didn't wait. She came running towards me,

hands out, hair falling down and the butler couldn't hide his disapproval.

'Nell, for goodness sake, what's happening?'

When I didn't respond she stopped short a few feet away from me.

'Are they all here?'

She nodded, biting her lip.

'Piggy Ditchbrake and his sister too?'

'Yes. I just went there and got him. Guggles is furious. And I sent a message to Louise early this morning. She arrived a few minutes ago.'

'What reason have you given them?'

'I said you knew Charles hadn't killed Migson. I said you knew who did. Was I right?'

'Yes.'

She took a long breath. She was trembling all over.

'We'd better go in,' I said.

I hadn't been in the library before. It was a light, eighteenth-century room, white busts of classical writers against apple-green walls, book spines the colour of honey-comb. There was a fire in the grate. Lord Penwardine was standing beside it looking grimmer than the bust of Cicero. His mother, elegant in church-going blue and grey, was sitting as upright as ever in a spindly armchair to the right of the fireplace, ankles neatly together, handbag at her feet. Louise, all in black, was sitting on an upright chair a long way from Lord Penwardine. Piggy sat uneasily on a sofa next to her, face pale and eyes bloodshot. He made some attempt to stand up when Bella and I came in, then caught a glance from Lord Penwardine and subsided hurriedly. Bella closed the door and sat down close to it on another upright chair, also a long way from Lord Penwardine. It made a triangle, with Lord Penwardine on the hearth rug at its apex, Bella and Louise at its other two points.

Nobody offered me a chair but Lord Penwardine made me a speech.

'You should know, Miss Bray, that I shall be sending a report of every word you say to my solicitor. I've no doubt at all about your purpose in coming here. It is, in collusion with my wife, to try to secure the release of a man justly

178

arrested for murder. Anything you say will be at best slander, at worst conspiracy to pervert the course of justice.'

I walked across a few yards of carpet so that I was facing Lord Penwardine and his mother by the fireplace, Louise and Piggy on my right, Bella on my left.

'I'm very happy, Lord Penwardine, for your solicitor or anybody else to know what I'm going to say. We might start with how you lied to the police when you said you were at home with your mother on the evening Migson was murdered. At least three people in this room know that isn't true: your wife, your mother and Piggy Ditchbrake.'

Piggy said: 'I didn't . . . she's . . .' Then trailed off into stutters. The fact was that he'd been so drunk the afternoon before that he couldn't remember what he'd told me. His sister gave him a hard look but Lord Penwardine didn't even glance at him.

I said: 'You should be grateful. You have two witnesses who can swear that they saw you outside the theatre at the time when Matthew Migson was shot inside. Otherwise you'd have been chief suspect.'

'Why should I have wanted to kill a man I'd never met?'

'The person who shot Migson in the back never intended to kill him. He was in Bella's costume, headgear as well. The light was bad. That shot was intended to kill your wife.'

I glanced at Bella. Her hands were clasped together, eyes on Penwardine.

'But however much you may have wanted to kill your wife, you didn't. And, as it turns out, she's your alibi for killing Migson. Just as I've been Piggy's alibi all along. Whoever shot Migson, it couldn't have been you or Piggy Ditchbrake. But it was somebody you were both very concerned about. Concerned enough for you to order Piggy to go back inside the theatre after he'd been thrown out, and for Piggy to go.'

I could sense the effort Lord Penwardine was making not to let his eyes move in a particular direction.

'I wondered who that might be,' I said. 'I should have known. I should have remembered something that happened on the day of the dress rehearsal, the day before the murder. It happened at the stage door at the Crispin Theatre.'

Silence. There was only one person in the room besides myself who knew what was coming. I didn't look at her.

'I should explain that stage door-keepers in the West End, wherever Charles Courts is playing, have got into the habit of taking money from his women admirers to let them secretly into dress rehearsals. I happened to catch the door-keeper at the Crispin letting a group of them out. We were talking about this when another woman arrived, claiming to be an admirer of Charles Courts. She hadn't been at the dress rehearsal or the door-keeper would have recognised her. In his job you must have a good memory for faces. What she wanted was Charles Courts' home address.'

I turned to Louise.

'But he wouldn't give it to you, would he, Miss Ditchbrake?'

She had nerve. Her lisping voice was level when she said, to Lord Penwardine and his mother, not to me:

'I'd decided that it had all gone on for too long. I wanted to find evidence myself that they were . . . committing misconduct together.'

There was no doubt that it came as a surprise to Lord Penwardine. He gasped, opened his mouth and closed it again.

'Who?' I asked her.

She said, with the clarity of a child at an elocution lesson:

'Lady Penwardine and Charles Courts. Everybody knew it but nobody seemed to be able to prove it.'

Bella said sharply: 'As it happens, that's a lie too. Mr Courts and I have never committed misconduct together, as you put it.' Then, with a glance at her husband, she added: 'More's the pity.'

Penwardine ignored her. His mother shifted slightly in her chair as if a draught of foul air had crept in under the door.

I said: 'But the next time I met Miss Ditchbrake, it wasn't Mr Courts' address she wanted.'

'No. You're not to tell them about that.'

It was the first sign of emotion from Louise since we'd started. There was a spot of red in her cheeks.

'I'm sorry, but I must. It explains so much.'

I turned back to Lord Penwardine.

'Miss Ditchbrake had been told that your wife had gone

back to live with you. She thought I had influence with Bella. She came to ask me to persuade her to move out again, to leave the two of you together. She said she'd always loved you. She said she wanted your son.'

The colour had drained from Louise's cheeks as quickly as it had come. She sat rigid and stiff-faced. I thought if Lord Penwardine had ever been worth anybody's love he'd have gone across to her then and put his arms round her. He didn't move. It was his mother who came to her defence.

'Miss Bray, this is infamous. Miss Ditchbrake has done nothing to deserve being subjected to this.'

'There's worse to come. I knew Miss Ditchbrake must be desperate to make this appeal to me. She was, because she knew by then that an innocent man had been killed in the attempt to give her a chance of bearing Lord Penwardine's son and heir. Killed in mistake for Bella. And now that crime was twice-over useless because not only was Bella alive, she'd gone back to her husband.'

'You've no proof of this.'

The protest from Lord Penwardine came too late and too lamely.

'We'll come to proof in a moment. For now, just visualise the scene. It's backstage, dim lighting, everything in confusion. A desperate woman has got in with a gun in her bag. Perhaps she never intended to kill Bella. Perhaps she thought she could scare her. But when she saw Bella standing there in her flying-away outfit with her back turned – or thought she did – the temptation was too much. She must have known as soon as the body fell and the hat came off that she'd killed the wrong person, but she kept her head. She managed to heave the body into the balloon basket, probably hide somewhere and get away when the play started again. It was Piggy who got caught, and he was there under your orders. Do you deny that you sent him to look for Miss Ditchbrake?'

'Mr Ditchbrake wasn't looking for Louise. He was looking for me.'

The voice was as calm as when we'd been discussing art galleries, but I caught the movement from the corner of my eye, flung myself at it. Just a little bit too late. She had the pistol out of her handbag and must have been firing it as I moved. The crash of the shot came a split second before I could shout a warning, followed by a yell from Bella.

It was a yell of fury, not of hurt. The smell of burnt powder and the echoes of the shot hung in the air as Bella came raging across the room.

'No.'

Lady Dorothea still had the pistol and was holding it steadily.

'Mother.'

Lord Penwardine's voice was hoarse. She looked at him and that gave me the moment I needed to knock the gun out of her hand.

'Really, Miss Bray, was that quite necessary?'

Bella's rush brought her cannoning into me.

'That bitch tried to shoot me.'

'Yes,' I said. 'For the second time.'

But I don't think anybody heard me because at that point Lord Penwardine acted for himself at last. It certainly wasn't the most effective action in the situation but probably it was something he'd been wanting to do for a long time. He walked up to Bella and, with the flat of his hand, struck her hard against the side of the face.

'Don't use language like that to my mother.'

Bella didn't make a sound. She stared at him wide-eyed and sat down on the nearest sofa, hand to her cheek.

The Dowager Marchioness of Penwardine, on her feet now, stared all round her, at Piggy and Louise, at Bella and me, as if we were the ones guilty of making an embarrassing scene.

'Yes, I shot the little man. I'd meant to shoot Isabella, of course, so it all seems rather a waste. George, I think you'd better do what has to be done and marry Louise as soon as possible.'

She turned to me.

'Did you bring a policeman with you, Miss Bray? If not, you may ask the butler to call one.'

Her pistol was lying there on the hearth rug, so I picked it up. It didn't seem to me to be the kind of job you should leave to the servants.

TWENTY-FIVE

TWO DAYS LATER. SCENE: BELLA'S study at her home in Berkeley Square. Charles, with the well-scrubbed look of somebody who was still trying to get the smell of prison off his skin, was sitting at one end of the violet-coloured sofa. Bella was at the other, but she kept glancing at him and having to restrain her hand when it strayed towards him. I'd dropped in, at Bella's request, on my way to Victoria Station to meet a couple of visiting suffragists from Switzerland.

'I thought it was Louise. I really thought you meant Louise.'

'That was the point. You all had to think I meant Louise.'

'But how did you know it wasn't her? It might have been her just as easily as his mother, up until the time she pulled the pistol on me.'

'No. There were three things that pointed to her.'

'Top up her mug, Charles. What three?'

Charles poured champagne into my tankard with an expert hand.

'First, if the killer mistook Migson for you, he or she had to be somebody who knew you'd be wearing a blue leather flying outfit. But it was only delivered before the dress rehearsal, so the only people who know about it would be the company, plus any outsider who happened to be at the dress rehearsal. And we know Louise wasn't there. She didn't appear till it was over.'

'But you didn't know Lady Dorothea was.'

'Not at first, though perhaps I should have guessed earlier. The door-keeper said he'd let "an old one on her own" into a box. Later, when I showed him the photograph of Lady Dorothea at the hunt ball, he identified her as the same woman. Perhaps she'd gone with the idea of shooting you there and then on stage, and lost her nerve for once.'

Unconsciously, Bella's hand went to her cheek.

'What was the second thing?'

'To mistake Migson for you, even from the back in bad light, the killer was probably short-sighted. That was the first thing I knew about Lady Dorothea. She had to use a lorgnette to look at me at my aunt's party. But Louise, I noticed, has very good eyesight. Then there was the matter of Lady Dorothea's bad back. You knew about that too, Charles.'

'Did I?'

'You remember when we were talking to the chauffeur in the mews. He mentioned that there'd been a delay when Lord Penwardine and his mother were going to the station because she had a bad back and the groom had to go and find a rug to make a pad for her. You might say a woman in her sixties might have a bad back in any case, but if that were so they'd have kept a cushion for her in the carriage as a matter of routine. Even though Migson wasn't a heavyweight as men go, it must have taken all the strength she could summon up to heave his body into that basket.'

A withdrawn look had come over Charles' face. By then he'd had to tell Bella about Migson's infatuation, but he didn't like to be reminded of him. Neither did she.

'And Louise really did come to you and beg you to get me to leave Guggles again?'

'Yes, though I thought at the time she was talking about Charles. She thought I knew more than I really did at that point. When I thought back to that talk with her, it finally convinced me that it was your mother-in-law who fired the shot. Lady Dorothea went to the theatre without Penwardine knowing about it and he must have been half mad with worry when he found out she was there. She was tired of waiting for other people to do things and had decided to take things into her own hands.'

'But how did that connect with what Louise said to you?'

184

'She told me she wanted to bear "his" son – he being Lord Penwardine. She added, "Even his mother wants me to have his son." At the time, thinking about Charles, I assumed it was sheer hysteria. But once I knew who she was it fell into place.'

Charles said: 'I don't see why . . .'

'Of course you do.' Bella swooped in. 'It was because I'd been a total disappointment to them in that department. When she saw she'd backed the wrong mare his mother shifted her bet to Louise. Only she still wanted my money for them. Isn't that right, Nell?'

She tried to speak jauntily but the hurt was there.

'Yes. I'm afraid Lady Dorothea was obsessed with the importance of handing on the family name. In comparison with that, your life or Migson's wasn't important. Or her own, come to that.'

Charles glanced at me. His short time in prison had been enough to show him what life would be like now for Lady Dorothea. That was something we had in common that Bella couldn't understand.

'I wish . . . No, I don't wish, I just wonder if it might have been different. If he'd ever loved me at all, or perhaps if I'd managed to deceive myself he did for a while longer, then perhaps I'd have had their heir for them and none of this would have happened. But he didn't, you see, not the least bit. She made him marry me.'

She blinked back tears. Charles' hand moved along the sofa, took hers and squeezed it.

'What will happen to her?'

'I think she'll plead guilty. Rather that than have everything come out in court.'

'And then . . .?'

'It will depend on the judge.'

Silence. When Bella spoke she was still subdued.

'I can divorce him now. He hit me before witnesses. That counts as cruelty.'

'Yes, I can't imagine he'll make any difficulties now. He's under orders from his mother to marry Louise. Under the settlement, as you're divorcing him I suppose you get your two million dollars back.'

185

'Yes.'

But she didn't sound as urgent as when we'd last talked about it. I asked Charles what he was going to do.

'I'm going to America. We were discussing it before all this happened. They want me to do *Romeo* in New York, then a tour, and perhaps I'll be able to get in some flying with the Wrights in my spare time. I'll miss Bella, but it will give things a chance to quieten down here. Then when the divorce comes through she'll join me and we'll get married.'

And live happily ever after.

'Will you be choosing your own cast for *Romeo*?'

'They're giving me a free hand.'

'You'll need a Mercutio. Why not take Vincent Colvin with you?'

It had come to me suddenly. I'd been thinking about the people who, through no fault of their own, had been harmed on the way to this final scene. I couldn't do anything for Migson, but here was something I might do. I liked Vincent, and he hadn't told Inspector Merit about Migson and Charles.

'You know, that's not a bad idea. His air of cynicism might be just right.'

'I should ask him soon, before he gets fixed up with something else. Now I must dash or my Swiss will go wandering.'

Charles came with me into the square. He couldn't stay the evening with Bella unchaperoned. He was still subdued from trying to keep up with things.

'I'm sorry your cheek got hurt.'

'I'm sorry about your aeroplane.'

'Arthur went to fetch it today.'

As we parted at the far side of the square a couple of girls came up and asked him for his autograph. He'd recover.

A month later. Scene: the office of Bella's solicitors in Lincoln's Inn. I'd gone there, for Bella again, to swear an affidavit saying I'd seen her husband strike her on the cheek. That act of violence was the key that would unlock Bella's marriage and her dollars. I'd been worried that I might have to go into details about what led up to the blow but the solicitor, who seemed to know most of what had happened, said it wouldn't be necessary. The other side were offering no counter evidence, anxious to see the divorce go through as soon as possible.

When the thing had been done, and I was putting on my coat and gloves, I asked the solicitor if he knew when Lady Penwardine's trial was scheduled.

'I've heard just this morning that the trial will not be taking place.'

'What?'

I thought that influence had done it again, that the Penwardines had somehow pulled enough strings to get away with murder.

'Lady Penwardine died last night in Holloway prison. Of pneumonia. I understand it came on quite suddenly, as it does sometimes with elderly people.'

I walked along streets hung with Christmas decorations, thinking about it. Pneumonia on the death certificate, but the real cause was surely that warped and ferocious will. Penwardines didn't hang.

More than two years later when, in the press of other events, I'd almost forgotten the Penwardine case, two things happened on the same day. In the morning I had a letter from Chicago, spilling excitement and happiness from every curlicue of its sprawling writing. It was signed Bella Courts. They were married. The *Romeo* tour had been a great success. Charles had retired from the stage and they were planning to set up an air company to transport cargoes between Chicago and New York. Charles had taught Bella to fly and 'I've only crashed twice, but one of those didn't count because the wing fell off'. I was cordially invited to come and stay with them and she'd take me up in her aeroplane – presumably with the wing back on it. In a postscript she added that Vincent Colvin had also been a great success as Mercutio and had decided to stay and act in New York. 'All the women there are going mad over him, like they did over Charles, but it doesn't seem to have turned his head at all.' I couldn't decide whether Bella was being tactful or naive, but it was good news in any case.

That afternoon I bumped into my aunt in Oxford Street. After an exchange of courtesies that made me feel like something being handled at arm's length between tweezers, she got down to the business of the Penwardines. She knew I'd been involved but had never been able to find out exactly how, which annoyed her.

'You know he married the little Ditchbrake girl? They did it as soon as the divorce became absolute, and not a moment too soon, it seems.'

'I'd heard.'

'The baby was born last week.'

'Oh, the son and heir at long last.'

Perhaps somewhere in the shades the ghost of Lady Penwardine was placated. My aunt glared at me.

'It's a girl.'

From the way she said it she blamed me for that as well.